Molly's Story

A Dog's Purpose Novel

Also by
W. Bruce Cameron

Bailey's Story
Ellie's Story
Molly's Story

A Dog's Purpose
A Dog's Journey
The Dogs of Christmas
A Dog's Way Home

Molly's Story

A Dog's Purpose Novel

W. Bruce Cameron

Illustrations by

Richard Cowdrey

A Tom Doherty Associates Book
New York

This is a work of fiction. All of the characters, organizations, and events portrayed
in this novel are either products of the author's imagination
or are used fictitiously.

MOLLY'S STORY: A DOG'S PURPOSE NOVEL

Copyright © 2017 by W. Bruce Cameron

A Starscape Book
Published by Tom Doherty Associates
175 Fifth Avenue
New York, NY 10010

www.tor-forge.com

The Library of Congress Cataloging-in-Publication Data
is available upon request.

ISBN 978-0-7653-9493-4 (hardcover)
ISBN 978-0-7653-9495-8 (ebook)

Our books may be purchased in bulk for promotional, educational, or business use.
Please contact your local bookseller or the Macmillan Corporate and Premium
Sales Department at 1-800-221-7945, extension 5442, or by email
at MacmillanSpecialMarkets@macmillan.com.

First Edition: July 2017

Printed in the United States of America

0 9 8 7 6 5 4 3 2 1

For Sadie.
Thanks for joining the party!

Molly's Story

A Dog's Purpose Novel

1

At first, everything was dark.

I felt warmth all around me, and I could smell other puppies cuddled up close. I could smell my mother, too. Her scent was safety, and comfort, and milk.

When I was hungry, I would squirm toward that smell, and find milk to drink. When I was cold, I would press close to her fur, or burrow under a brother or a sister. And then I'd sleep until I was hungry again.

When I opened my eyes after a few days, things began to get more interesting.

I could see now that my mother's fur was short and curly and dark. Most of my brothers and sisters looked like that, too. Only one had fur like mine, as dark as my mother's, but straight and soft, with no curl to it at all.

9

One day, after my stomach was full, I didn't fall asleep right away. Instead, I stood up and braced myself on wobbly legs. I took a few steps, and my nose bumped into something smooth, with a funny, dry smell. I licked it. It tasted dry, too, and not nearly as interesting as licking my mother or the other puppies nearby.

I was pretty worn out by all this excitement, so I pushed my way underneath the sleeping body of a sister and took a nap. Later on, I ventured a little farther. On every side was more of that cardboard. It was under my feet, too. We were in a box.

Sometimes a woman came to lean over the box and talk to us. I'd blink up at her sleepily. Her voice was kind, and her hands, when they came down to pet us, were gentle. My mother would thump her tail, letting me know that this woman was a friend.

One day she slid her hands right under my belly and hoisted me up into the air.

"You need a name," she told me, holding me close to her nose. I tasted it with my tongue, and she giggled. "You're sweet, that's for sure. How about Molly? You look like a Molly to me. Want to explore? Those legs are getting strong." She plopped me down on a new surface, wrinkly and soft. I put my nose down to it eagerly. I could smell soap, and soft cotton fuzz, and other dogs. I nibbled it. The woman laughed.

"It's not to eat, silly girl. Here, maybe you need some

company. I think I'll call this one Rocky." Another puppy, one of my brothers, landed on the blanket next to me. He was the only one who looked like me, with short hair. He tilted his head to one side, studied me, sneezed, and chewed on my ear.

I shook him off and headed off to find out more about this new space.

It was shockingly huge. I could take many, many steps at a time. I was astounded at how much room there was in the world! By the time my nose bumped into a new pair of shoes, I was worn out. I barely had energy to get my teeth around a shoelace and tug.

The owner of the shoes bent down to pull the shoelace out of my mouth. I growled, to show her it was mine.

"So adorable!" the person with the shoelace said. "Is she a poodle, Jennifer?"

"Half," said the woman who'd taken me out of the box. Jennifer, I guessed, must be her name. "Mom's a standard poodle, definitely. But the dad—who knows? Spaniel, maybe? Terrier?"

"How many did she have?"

"Seven," said Jennifer. "She was pregnant when I found her. After the pups are weaned, I'll see about taking her in to get her spayed. Then I'll find her a home."

"And homes for all of these puppies, too?" asked the owner of the shoelace. "We'll take that one over there, but we can't have more than that." She scooped me up in soft hands and returned me to the box, where I nestled close to my mother and had a little snack.

"Of course. I understand," Jennifer said. "Not to worry. I've been fostering dogs a long time. The right home usually comes along at the right time."

She stroked my head as I curled up for a nap, right next to my mother where I belonged.

After that, Jennifer came to take us out of the box more and more often. I got a chance to explore the living room, pounce on a couch cushion to teach it who was boss, and even peek out into a hallway where the floor was so slippery and slick that my feet went out from under me. A sister tried to climb on me when I was down, but she couldn't get any traction with her back feet on the slick floor, so that didn't work. All I had to do was roll over and shake her off.

That's when I caught the scent of another dog in the air.

My head went up. My ears went up, too. I got to my feet, staring and sniffing hard. At the far end of the hallway, a big dog was standing, watching me.

"Barney? Be nice to the new pups," Jennifer said.

Barney was very tall, much taller than my mother, and I could smell that he was male. He had astonishingly long ears that hung down beside his face and swung back and forth when he put his head down closer to the ground.

I was fascinated. I didn't have ears like that, and my

mother didn't, either. Neither did my brothers and sisters. I set off to investigate. My sister stayed behind me and whimpered a little for our mother to come and save her. But I was ready to find out more.

With each step, my feet tried to skid away from me. My claws were no help at all; they couldn't get any kind of grip on the polished wood. But I pressed on, and soon I was right up close to the new dog.

Barney put his giant muzzle down to the ground. It was as big as my whole body! He sniffed at my face. Then he sniffed along my whole body, nudging me so hard with his nose that I lost my balance and sat down. But I held still. He was bigger and older, and I knew that it was my job to stay quiet and let him do what he liked.

"Good dog, Barney," Jennifer said.

His nose came back to my head. He let out a snuffly sigh and turned to walk away.

His long, droopy, silky ears swung back and forth, back and forth. And I just couldn't resist.

I jumped forward and snatched at one of those ears with my teeth.

Barney snorted and pulled his head away. I held on. It was tug-of-war! I couldn't bite very hard yet, with my weak jaws, but already I loved playing this game. I'd do it with my brothers and sisters in the box whenever we found anything we could chew. I'd never played it with anything as wonderful as a long, soft, dangling ear.

"Molly, no!" called Jennifer, trying to sound stern. But she was laughing. Barney backed away, looking confused. He towed me with him, my teeth still in his ear. Then he shook his big head, and I tumbled over in a somersault, ending up flat on the floor with all four of my legs splayed out in different directions.

Barney snorted again and began to walk away. I charged up, ready to chase him and get that ear again. But Jennifer scooped me up before I could manage it and settled me back in the box with my littermates.

It wasn't fair because I knew that if I set my feet I could really give that ear a good tug, but a big meal and some sleep took my mind off the injustice.

As my siblings and I grew bigger, our box seemed to become smaller and smaller, and our mother wanted more time away from us. Jennifer started taking us outside more and more often to play.

I *loved* outside. It was wonderful.

There was grass to chew, with a fascinating juicy taste that was not like anything inside the house. There were sticks that tasted even better. Birds flitted overhead. Once I scratched in the dirt and found a worm twisting and coiling between my claws. I nosed it with delight until a brother knocked me away and the worm squirmed back into the earth again while I dealt with my littermate.

Barney did not come outside much. He liked to spend most of his days asleep on a soft bed in a corner of one of the inside rooms. But there was another dog, named Che, who barely came inside at all, except to eat. Che was big and gray, and he loved to run. And it was even better if he were being chased.

The very first time I went outside, he dashed over to where I was sitting next to Rocky. Che bowed down low on his front paws, his back legs high in the air, his tail beating back and forth. Then he jumped up again and ran away, looking at us to see if we'd figured it out.

Rocky and I sat staring at him. What did he want?

Che seemed to decide that we didn't understand. He came back and bowed again. Then he dashed off once more.

Rocky seemed fascinated by Che's plumy tail. He set off after it, and I set off after Rocky. It would not be right if he had fun without me.

Che raced in a big circle around the yard so fast he came up behind us. I jumped around to stare at him. Rocky yipped.

Che bowed again and tore off. We followed, running as fast as we could on our short, clumsy legs. It seemed the right thing to do. Every time we came outside after that, Che was there, begging us to chase him. We always obliged.

But Che did not stay long at Jennifer's. One day a woman came to visit, and she took Che home with her. "It's wonderful, what you do," she said to Jennifer as she

stood by the gate to the yard, with Che on a leash beside her. "I think if I tried to foster dogs I'd wind up keeping all of them."

Jennifer laughed. "That's called 'foster failure,' Mrs. Kutner. It's how I ended up with Barney. He was my first foster. I realized, though, that if I didn't get control of myself I'd adopt a few dogs and then that'd be it, and I wouldn't be able to help any others."

"Come, Che!" the new woman said, and she tugged at the leash. Tail wagging, Che bounded after her. They went through the gate, and it shut behind them.

Che was gone.

2

I dashed over to the gate and put my paws up against it. I yipped as loudly as I could. Where was Che? Wasn't he coming back? Who would we chase now?

Jennifer came over and stroked my head. "It's okay, Molly," she said softly. "Dogs find the right people and go to live with them. It's what's supposed to happen."

I didn't understand her words, but her touch felt comforting. I let her stroke me for a while, and then I hurried over to my mother and burrowed into her soft warmth. She licked me, and I felt better.

Still, it was hard to understand what had happened to Che. I was glad I wasn't going anywhere. That I'd always stay in this yard with Jennifer and Rocky and my other brothers and sisters and my mother.

A few days later, a new dog arrived. Rocky and I were playing in the backyard when Jennifer brought her in through the gate.

I sat up, with Rocky's paw still in my mouth, to look at her. She was very thin and had light brown eyes, nearly the same color as her fur.

"Pups, this is Daisy," Jennifer said. She put down a hand to unclip Daisy's leash from her collar. Daisy shied away from her hand. As soon as she was free, Daisy dashed to hide under a picnic table. She seemed to feel safer there.

My mother came over to give the new dog a good sniff. Daisy held still and then did the same back. She wasn't shy with Rocky or me, either. When we came over, Daisy stuck her nose down to be sniffed, and even flopped down so we could wrestle with her. I liked Daisy, I decided. Wrestling was even more fun than chasing.

But when Jennifer came outside with bowls of food and water, Daisy waited until Jennifer was far away before she bolted over to the food and devoured it in three gulps.

"Good girl," Jennifer said softly from the steps to the house, where she had sat down to watch Daisy eat. "You'll get used to nice people, sweetie. It won't take long. Want to go hide some more now?"

Daisy licked her bowl clean and dashed back under the picnic table, just as the gate to the street clicked open and two new people came in. Neither one was as tall as Jennifer. One was male and one was female—I could smell that. Both were laughing.

They were young, I realized. Sort of like human puppies. A boy and a girl.

This was interesting.

"So cute!" the girl exclaimed. She dropped to her knees and spread her arms wide. I knew just what that meant. My mother stayed near the picnic table with Daisy, but I raced right over to the girl, with Rocky at my side.

There was something about this girl—about the warm smell of her skin and her hair, about the sound of her laughter as she lifted me up and held me close to her face, about the taste of toast and butter and honey that lingered on her mouth where I licked her. This girl was special.

This girl, I decided, was mine.

Excitement spread through me, and I couldn't hold still. I wiggled until the girl put me down, and then I danced and spun on the grass, my little tail beating the air. I raced away from the girl, turning in a circle, and ran back to lick her hands and listen to her laugh some more.

The boy who stood next to her was laughing, too.

"Come on, come on!" he called, and he ran a few steps. Even without the play bow that Che used, it was pretty clear what he wanted. Rocky raced after him and jumped on his tennis shoes.

"What do you think, Trent?" the girl asked.

"He's great!" the boy replied.

Normally, I loved to chase, too, but I stayed close to the girl this time, squirming to get close to her face, licking her under the chin.

"Molly seems pretty smitten with you," Jennifer said to the girl. "I'll be right back. You get to know the pups a little."

Jennifer went inside, but the girl stayed close to me. That was right. That was just what she should do. "Oh, you are so cute," the girl said, smoothing my ears back. I kissed her fingers. "But my mom would never let me have a dog," she told me. "I just came with Trent."

The boy scooped up Rocky and came back with him. "Look, CJ, see his paws? He's going to be bigger than that one. What's her name?"

"Molly," CJ said. I wiggled with pleasure to hear her say my name. She got to her feet, and I stood on my back legs and stretched my forepaws up as high as I could against her jeans until she picked me up.

She had warm brown eyes and a scattering of freckles across her face. I leaned into her arms, looking into those eyes.

And I understood something new. I was supposed to take care of this girl. That was my job.

Maybe that was why Che had left the yard! Maybe the woman he'd gone with was *his* person, and he was meant to take care of her, just the way I would take care of this girl. CJ, that was her name. CJ was my girl, and I was going to look after her the best that I possibly could.

I felt a pang at my heart to think of going away from the yard, and my mother, and everything I'd known, but as long as I could snuggle close to CJ, it would be okay.

"I want him," the boy said. "Rocky, you want to come home with me?" Rocky squirmed to get out of his arms, and Trent gently dropped him to the grass. Rocky jumped on a rubber bone and shook it.

"This is so exciting!" CJ said. She let me down gently, too. "You're so lucky, Trent." She tried to pet Rocky, but I wiggled between them and thrust my head under her hand. She laughed.

"Molly likes you," Trent said.

"I know." Somehow there was a little sadness in the girl's voice. How funny that she was sad when we were together! I got my teeth into her sock and tugged at it.

"But Gloria," the girl went on. "I can practically hear her. She hates dogs. 'They're so *filthy*. They *lick*.' She'd never let me have one."

"It would be fun, though," Trent said. He sounded a little sad, too. "We'd have a brother and a sister."

"Yeah." CJ dropped to her knees, tugged her sock out from between my teeth, and held my face in her hands. "Yeah, it would be fun. Oh, Molly, I'm sorry, girl."

I licked her nose.

Jennifer came back out, smiling to see Trent with Rocky, and me with CJ. "Are there papers or anything to fill out?" Trent asked.

"Nope. I'm not an official shelter or anything. I'm just the neighborhood lady who everybody knows will take in strays and find them homes."

"So it's okay for me to take Rocky?" Trent picked up my brother and tucked him under his chin.

"More than okay. Just, please, if for any reason it's not working out, bring him back."

"Oh, it's going to work out great. Rocky? Ready to go to your new home?" the boy asked, grinning.

CJ set me down on the grass. I sat and scratched my ear and waited for her to pick me back up.

"Oh, look at her," CJ said. "It's like she knows I'm leaving without her."

"Come on, CJ," Trent said. "We'd better go."

The four of us—the boy and his dog, my girl and me—headed over toward the gate.

I paused to glance back at my mother, still sitting by the picnic table. And I hesitated. She lay down, setting her head on her paws, and steadily looked at the two of us. I felt as if she were telling me it was all right. That I was doing what I was meant to do. Dogs had to leave their mothers, and sometimes their first homes, to do their jobs. To take care of their people.

I had to take care of CJ. It was time to go.

Jennifer opened the gate. Rocky and Trent went through. CJ followed. I kept close at her heels.

"No, Molly," Jennifer said, sticking out her foot to block me.

The gate swung shut.

I sat down and stared at it.

I was on one side of the wooden gate, and my girl was on the other. That was not right! It was not how things should be!

"It's okay, Molly," Jennifer said.

I yipped, frustrated that my voice was so tiny. How would my girl hear me? I jumped past Jennifer and put my tiny claws up on the gate and scratched at it. CJ could not leave without me! I had to go with her!

But the gate did not open. CJ was gone. Rocky was gone. I barked and barked with my useless little puppy voice. Jennifer was here, my mother was here, my new friend Daisy was here. But I still felt all alone in the world.

3

Daisy came over and sniffed me as I barked. She understood that I was unhappy; I could see that. But she did not understand why. Some humans had left the yard. Why was that a problem? Daisy seemed happier, in fact, with fewer people around.

I tried to bite at the bottom of the gate, but all that did was hurt my teeth. I ran to my mother, and she licked me affectionately from nose to rump, but that was no help, either. I needed my girl!

"Molly?"

The sound of her voice jolted me. I turned and yipped once more. There she was. CJ. She was standing just inside the open gate.

Jennifer was next to her, smiling.

CJ dropped to her knees. I ran over and threw myself into her arms, licking her face, burrowing my nose under her chin. It had all been an awful mistake. Thank goodness! I'd thought for a moment that my girl was actually going to leave me!

CJ looked up at Jennifer, and at Trent, who came back into the yard, too, holding Rocky in his arms. "She chose me, so what could I do? Molly chose me," CJ insisted.

I was happy to be Molly. I was happy to be with CJ. She held me close as she talked with Jennifer and then carried me out through the gate. I was with my girl, feeling her gentle hands around me, snuggling close to the warmth of her skin. Everything would be all right after all.

"So what *is* your mom going to say?" Trent asked. On the sidewalk there was a wagon with a cardboard box inside it. Trent put Rocky gently in the box. CJ set me next to him. Rocky jumped on me happily, his tail wagging, as if we'd been apart for days. Obviously, the only thing to do next was wrestle.

The wagon started to bump down the sidewalk. Trent was pulling it. CJ was walking next to him. I had my front legs on top of Rocky, but my back legs kept slipping off.

"CJ? Seriously?" he asked.

"I don't know," my girl said.

I barked to let her know I could hear her. She put a hand in the box and stroked my ears.

"Will she let you keep Molly?"

"Well, what am I supposed to do? You saw what happened. Molly and I are supposed to be together."

"Yeah, but it's not like your mom isn't going to notice that there's suddenly a dog around," Trent said.

CJ sighed. I licked at her fingers. I'd already figured out that being licked by a dog can cheer up just about anybody.

"CJ? You seriously think you can *hide a dog*? In your *house*?" Trent asked.

"I could hide a pack of wolves in the house if I wanted to," CJ said stubbornly. "Gloria doesn't even know if I'm there a lot of the time. She'd hardly notice a little puppy."

"Okay, sure. So for the next six years, until you go to college, you're going to hide a dog in your house and somehow your mom won't find out."

CJ sighed again. "You know what, Trent? Sometimes you don't do stuff because it makes sense. You just do it. Okay?"

"Right. That makes sense."

"You always have to argue with me."

They were both silent for a moment. Rocky had taken advantage of my time licking CJ to chew on my tail, so I had to teach him a lesson. Then I heard Trent speak up again.

"I'm sorry. I was just looking out for you," he said.

"Yeah, I know. But, um, go past my driveway, okay?" CJ said. "Just keep walking."

The two of them walked a little farther, and the wagon bumped a little more, and I fell over on Rocky and ended up with his head under my belly. Then CJ reached into the box and picked me up.

I looked down at my brother, who sat with his head cocked, looking up at me. It was good-bye; I knew that somehow. Just as I'd said good-bye to my mother and Daisy and Jennifer and the yard, I was going to say good-bye to my brother now. But it was all right, because I'd be with my girl. My girl who needed me.

"You sure it'll be—" Trent started to say.

"It'll be fine, Trent," CJ said firmly. And she turned around and started walking. I heard the wagon with Rocky in it rattle and bump away as CJ carried me down the sidewalk toward a house. Some dogs had marked the bushes outside, but the scents were old. Nothing told me that any other dogs lived here now.

"Okay," CJ told me, her voice low. "Let's see how quiet you can be."

Moving quickly now, she carried me through a front door, up some stairs, down a hall, and into a bedroom. I cuddled into her warmth, tired now from all of the barking and worrying and the excitement of the wagon ride down the street.

"Clarity? Is that you?" a woman called from some-where inside the house.

"I'm home!" CJ yelled. Her voice was so loud that I twitched and yipped a little, and she shushed me, her hand rubbing along my back. Then she set me down on a bed.

The surface under my paws was soft and padded. It felt nothing like a wooden floor, or a cardboard box, or springy grass. I took a step and fell over, struggling back to my feet. When CJ sat down on the bed beside me, I fell over again.

CJ giggled. "Oh, Molly!" She reached out to pick me up, and I licked her hands enthusiastically. My girl tasted delicious.

Then we both heard footsteps in the hall. CJ froze.

"Molly! Shhh!" she said. Then she flopped down on the bed and yanked a billowy pink-and-yellow quilt over her, bending her knees to make a tented space. She snatched me and shoved me into that space. It was dim and warm in there, and I was surrounded by sheets that smelled like my girl. What a wonderful game!

"Ta-daa!" a woman's voice sang.

"Gloria? You bought that?" CJ asked, shocked.

"Of course!" said the other voice.

"A *fur*?"

Obviously, I was supposed to get out from under the sheets. I ducked out from under CJ's knees and began to struggle up toward her head, wading over soft bulges in the cotton sheets, shoving with my head to push past with the weight of the quilt that had settled down over me.

"You like? It's fox."

"A *fur*? How could you?"

CJ's hand came under the blankets, pushing me back down. I wrestled with it a bit, then licked at her fingers.

"Well, it's not like I killed anything. It was already dead when I bought the coat. And I need it for my trip. Aspen is the only place left where you can wear a fur without feeling guilty. And, well, probably France."

"Aspen? When are you going to Aspen?" CJ asked. She pulled her hand away. I did my best to chase after it.

"Monday. *So*, I was thinking, we should go shopping that morning, before I leave. Just the two of us."

"Monday's a school day," CJ said.

"Well, *school*. It's just a day."

CJ wiggled out from under the blankets, and the quilt settled softly down around my head. "I need a yogurt," CJ said.

I shook my entire body hard, staggered a few more steps, and poked my head out from under the quilt. I'd won! At last! But I was too late. CJ was already leaving the room, closing the door behind her.

"I hate it when you wear those shorts," I heard Gloria say from the hall. "They make your thighs look so heavy."

I was alone. Again! But last time my girl had come

back to me. That's what she'd do this time. I was sure of it.

Even so, it was hard to wait. I poked my nose over the side of the bed and decided that it was way too far for me to jump. So I paced back and forth, with difficulty, on the soft, lumpy quilt. I whimpered. I chewed on a stuffed toy, which helped a little.

Then the door opened. My girl!

"Good girl, Molly," she whispered, scooping me up.

Her breath had a lovely, sweet, milky scent. I licked her mouth and face eagerly, and she giggled and kissed me back. Then she pushed me deep into the soft shirt she was wearing.

I figured this was another game and tried to squirm out. I wanted to lick my girl's face some more and hear her laughing! But before I could do that, I felt her carrying me back down the stairs, and then we were in another yard. I knew it by the smells of grass and dirt and fresh, warm air, even before CJ pulled me out of her shirt.

The first thing I did when I got on the grass was to squat and pee. CJ seemed happy with that. She stroked me and talked to me, and then she tugged a plastic bag out of one of her pockets. Inside were some bits of cold, salty meat.

She offered me some, and I gobbled them up eagerly. But the salty flavor was so strong it burned my tongue! I shook my head to make the taste go away. Then I ate more. I was hungry by now, so hungry I almost didn't mind how the meat tasted. I just gulped it down.

"I'll get you some puppy food tomorrow, Molly, I promise," CJ said. "I promise, promise, promise. Do you want some more ham?"

I did. And that night I slept in the crook of CJ's arm. "I love you, Molly. I love you," she whispered as I drifted off to sleep.

I was so worn out by everything that had happened that day that I didn't even get up once. But by the time the sun was out, my little bladder was nearly bursting. Luckily, CJ got up early as well, putting on her clothes and carrying me outside. She talked to me in hushed whispers as I squatted and left a puddle that rapidly soaked into the grass.

Then she picked me up again and brought me inside. I figured we were about to go back up to her room for some more of that hiding-in-the-sheets game, but instead she carried me down some different stairs to a basement.

There were a lot of new smells. I hung over CJ's arm, my nose twitching as I tried to take them all in. Dampness . . . and wet earth . . . and old cement . . . and soap . . . and cardboard . . . and other things I was curious to explore.

CJ set me down. I sniffed around with interest. There were newspapers on the floor, and some cardboard beneath them. CJ crouched beside me, and fed me some more of that cold, salty ham.

"This is my special space here under the stairs, Molly," she whispered. "I got it all set up for you last night. See? Here's a pillow for you, and here's some water. You just have to be quiet, okay? I have to leave for just a bit. I promise I'll come back soon. Now don't bark. Be quiet, Molly. Be quiet."

CJ moved very suddenly, wiggling backward and jumping to her feet. She tried to pull a box across the floor to block me in, but I was too quick for that. She wasn't going to win this game! I darted out and jumped on her feet, wagging hard.

"Molly!" CJ groaned.

I put my front paws up on her legs and wagged harder. But to my surprise, she didn't laugh. With one hand, she pushed me back into the small, dark space I'd just escaped. And once again she pulled that box to block me in.

This time I wasn't fast enough. My nose bumped into the cardboard.

I thought I'd made my feelings clear when we were at Jennifer's. CJ was my person. I did not want to be left in this space. I wanted to be with CJ!

"Be good, Molly," CJ's voice said from the other side of the boxes. "Remember, stay quiet. Don't bark."

I sat down in dismay. What was all this about? Where

was my girl? I scratched at the boxes, but could not get them to move. I paced about, stepping in my water dish. I found a stray bit of ham on the floor and ate it, and the burn on my tongue reminded me to dash back to the water dish and lap some of it down.

My girl would come back. Of course she would. She had not left me in Jennifer's yard. She had not left me in the bedroom. She would come back for me this time, too.

But I wished she could understand that we should *always* be together!

I took a quick nap. I found a round ball just a little bit too big to go into my mouth, and I chewed on it as best I could. Then I had to squat and leave a puddle in a corner. The smell of my own urine was not particularly interesting, and I began to feel that I had waited long enough.

I barked, making my voice as loud as I could. The tiny space I was trapped in bounced the barks back at me, making it sound like there were at least two sad, bored, lonely puppies trapped down here. But even then, it wasn't very loud.

Still, now that I'd started barking, it seemed like a good idea to keep it up for a while. Then a new sound came to my ears, and I stopped.

I'd never heard anything like it before. It didn't sound like words, or barks, or even the noise a car makes rushing down the street. It was a human noise; I was pretty sure about that. But it was something between crying and wailing. Did humans howl when they were upset? Was a human somewhere in pain?

It was awful. I paced and whined. The dreadful noise got louder, and I heard heavy footsteps on the basement stairs. It wasn't CJ coming back to me—I could tell. A strange scent—flowery and oily at once—drifted around the boxes that held me in. Was the scent connected to that bewildering noise? I crouched low, worried, and whimpered as quietly as I could.

Overhead, I heard the front door open and shut. Then the basement door opened, too.

"Gloria? Are you down there?" It was CJ's voice, loud enough to hear over the wailing.

Relief spread through me. I didn't quite dare jump up and bark with joy, but I wagged my tail hard.

Footsteps came rattling down the stairs. "Gloria?" CJ's voice called, louder.

There was a loud scream. I jumped. CJ screamed, too. I squirmed back into the darker corner of my space. What was happening?

"Clarity June, you scared me to death!" Gloria gasped.

"Why didn't you answer? What are you doing?" CJ asked.

"I was singing! I had my earbuds in! What's in that bag?"

"It's dog food. We're, um, we're having a food drive at school."

"Do you really think it looks good to bring people dog food?"

"Mo-*ther*. It's not for the people. It's for their dogs. Dogs need help sometimes, too. Are you getting laundry? I'll help you fold," CJ offered. "Come on, let's take it upstairs."

CJ and Gloria went back up the stairs, leaving me alone. I bounced up and scratched at the boxes some more, harder this time, panting with anxiety and impatience.

How could CJ have come back, but left me here? Didn't she know I needed her?

Plus, I was getting very, very hungry.

4

What could have been a whole day passed. I'm not sure it was really a full day, but it was a *long* time before I heard footsteps on the basement stairs again.

I smelled CJ. I smelled food, too. How wonderful! CJ *and* food!

She pushed the boxes aside, and I leaped out, wriggling, and clambered onto her lap. Then I fell off again so I could bury my nose in the bowl of food she set down.

"She's finally gone. She went to do errands," CJ said. "Oh, Molly, I am so, *so* sorry."

I was too busy eating to do more than swipe briefly at her hand with my tongue. The little pieces inside the bowl were crunchy and tasty, and they didn't burn my tongue like the ham. I ate as quickly as I could, and then slurped up water while CJ picked up the damp newspaper I had left under the stairs and laid down some dry sheets. Then she opened a new door, one that led directly from the basement to the yard, and took me outside.

I *loved* the yard. It didn't have other dogs like Che or Barney or Daisy, but it did have grass, and dirt, and ants and beetles to chase, and sticks to chew, and worms to dig up. And of course it had CJ.

I sprawled on the warm grass, rolling in sheer joy. CJ flopped down beside me. How exciting! Jennifer had been nice, but she had never gotten down in the grass and rolled with me!

CJ and I played Tug on a Towel for a few minutes, but it had been a long morning for me, and I was exhausted. She scooped me up and held me close, and I fell asleep in her lap.

When I woke up, I was back in the dark, small space under the stairs.

I yipped impatiently. This was not where I wanted to be! CJ seemed to understand, for a few minutes later I heard her feet clattering down the stairs.

She shoved the boxes aside. "Shhh, Molly! You need to be quiet!" she said. "If my mother finds out you're here, she'll make me give you away!"

I thought I was beginning to understand my girl. When I wanted her, I should bark, and she would come.

She took me out of the corner, and I explored the basement a little, sniffed in dark corners, and got cobwebs stuck on my nose that CJ gently took off. When I needed to squat on the cement floor, she only laughed and shook her head and cleaned the puddle up. Then she hugged me and kissed me up and down my face. Love flowed from her, so strong that I wiggled all over with happiness.

We played and played outside until I was sleepy, and I didn't mind too much when she put me back under the stairs. I knew she'd come if I barked for her. Instead, I took another long nap. CJ had to wake me up when she came down for me in the middle of the night and took me outside to play and wrestle in the cool air of the backyard.

"Shhh, Molly," she kept saying. "Shhh!"

It probably meant she was as happy as I was to be outside together.

The next morning I woke up under the stairs again, listening to some strange, loud noises from upstairs. It sounded like more of that yowling, but in different voices this time. I heard Gloria talking, too. "Would you please turn down that music?" she asked.

I barked and scratched at the boxes that blocked my exit, ready to get out and play with CJ. But for some reason my girl was slow to come.

Then I heard a sigh of air as the door that connected

the basement and the yard opened up. The boxes slid away, and I jumped out, into CJ's arms. She was wearing jeans and a sparkly T-shirt, and she had a backpack on her back. I lapped at her chin, my heart beating fast with joy. Time to have some more fun!

"She's still eating breakfast," CJ whispered to me. "You have to be quiet, Molly. You can do that, right, girl?"

She set down a bowl filled with food for me, and another with water, so I figured she was asking if I wanted to eat. Of course I did! When I'd finished, my girl picked me up and carried me outside to the yard and through the gate out onto the street. Then she started to run, bouncing me up and down in her arms. It was not very comfortable. Tug on a Towel or Find That Worm were better games. But at least we were together.

When we reached a park, CJ let me down. The park was *wonderful*. Even better than the yard!

There was so much grass to run in, and flowers to bite, and chittering squirrels in the branches of trees overhead. I got dizzy watching them and racing from tree to tree, trying to track their movements. There was excellent dirt to scratch up, and I could smell that many other dogs had been there before me. When I was done running and scratching and smelling, I could always go and flop down on my girl's lap, and feel her scratching my back and running her gentle fingers along my ears.

We spent the morning in the park together, CJ and

41

me. After we had played for a long time, CJ took a cloth sack out of her backpack. It had lunch for both of us.

She took a bowl out of her backpack, too, and gave me more of the crunchy food. For herself, she had some of that ham stuffed inside bread. And she poured water from a bottle into her hand and let me lap up as much as I wanted.

After lunch I took a long nap with CJ stretched out on the grass beside me. When I woke, I found a likely looking stick and carried it back to my girl so that I could get petted and chew at the same time. CJ obliged. Then she stopped rubbing my ears so that she could wave. "Trent, hi!" she called. "Over here!"

I could tell she was not talking to me, so I didn't look up from my stick. Then, to my complete surprise, something about my size barreled into me and knocked me over.

My whole head was buried in soft fur that smelled familiar. It was my brother! It was Rocky!

I had thought, when we'd left Jennifer's yard together, that I would never see Rocky again. Somehow I'd had the feeling that was what happened, that dogs left their mothers and their littermates in order to be with their people. But here Rocky was, rolling me over in the grass, and I was so glad to see him that I jumped on his head and chewed his ears with delight.

CJ and Trent were sitting on the grass, laughing. "Do they remember each other? Do you think?" Trent asked.

"Of course they do!" my girl said, giggling. "Look at how happy they are."

"Did your mom leave on her trip?" Trent asked. "You know you could have stayed with us while she's gone. My mom would have said yes."

"She's leaving this afternoon," CJ said. "I just have to keep Molly at the park until then. And I don't mind staying by myself. It's not like I've never done it before. Besides, I've got Molly now."

"Yeah, you do." Trent sounded worried, but I was too busy pinning Rocky down to pay much attention. "But Gloria will be back in two days, CJ!"

"I *know* that. Trent, just . . . not now, okay? Look at the puppies. Let's just have fun."

After some playtime, Trent picked up Rocky and said good-bye, and CJ scooped me up, too, and carried me home. She finally seemed to have learned that the space under the stairs was not a good spot for dogs, because we went in the front door together, and she let me down on the living room floor.

I was so happy to be beside my girl in our own house that I could have raced in circles, barking and wagging. But I was pretty tired from our morning at the park, so all I did was flop down on CJ's feet and pant happily.

She scooped me up and lay down on the couch, holding me close. I wedged my head under her chin.

I sighed with pleasure and fell asleep.

That evening CJ fed me dinner in the living room. We sat on the floor, not far from the fireplace. She ate another ham sandwich while she watched pictures that flickered on a flat piece of glass, a screen. When a dog barked from the direction of that screen, I sat up straight, pricking my ears. Was there another dog in this house somewhere?

"Silly Molly," said CJ affectionately. She fed me a bit of ham. It tasted even better when she handed me small pieces, because I could feel her love, plus there was fresh ham-taste on her fingers every time. "It's just you and me. You know what? I actually like it better when she's gone. Especially with you here, girl. You're going to keep me company."

I squatted down and made a puddle on the floor, which made CJ sit straight up on the couch and drop her sandwich. So I helped myself to bits of it while she ran to get soft, square pieces of paper to dab at the carpet with. Then she took me outside.

I slept in CJ's bed that night, and I was so happy about this that I kept waking up and licking her face. She would bat my nose away, but I could tell she didn't really mean it. Finally, I settled down to nibble on her fingers whenever I felt that I just had to show her how much I loved her, and that's how we spent the night.

The next day CJ stood by the stove and made scrambled eggs, putting some in a bowl for me. Delicious! When we went out into the backyard, it was raining, so we didn't stay long. CJ petted me and praised me when I emptied my bladder and bowels into the grass, and I licked at her hands. Whatever made my girl happy made me happy.

We played in the house that day, just her and me. "Come here, Molly!" she called when we were back inside, and I followed her down the hallway.

She opened a door, and we went into a room I had not seen before. There was that smell again, flowery and oily with the warmth of a grown-up woman mixed in. I knew that was Gloria's smell, and looked around for her, but she was nowhere to be seen.

"Here, Molly," CJ called. "See the dog in the mirror?"

I heard the word "dog" and trotted up to her. Then I jumped back. There was another dog in here!

It looked just like Rocky, but what was it doing inside my house? I bounded forward, and then pulled back in surprise as the other dog jumped fiercely at me.

It didn't smell like Rocky. In fact, it didn't smell like a dog at all. Confused, I wagged my tail. It wagged. I bowed down to see if it wanted to play. It bowed down, too.

I barked. It looked like it was barking back, but it didn't make any noise. Very strange!

"Say hi, Molly! Get the dog!" CJ said.

I crept closer to the other dog, sniffing hard. How strange. It must not be a dog after all, just something that looked like a dog.

"You see the dog, Molly? See the dog?"

Whatever was going on, it wasn't very interesting. I turned away, snuffling along the floor to see what I could discover. CJ was looking at the place where we'd seen the dog-that-was-not-a-dog, pulling her fingers through her hair.

I sniffed under the bed. It smelled dusty under there. I poked my nose in farther, and it bumped into something. I got my teeth into the thing and pulled it out. It had a promising smell, like sweat and dirt and something animal-like. It felt good in my mouth, too. I settled down to give it a good chew as CJ fiddled with her hair. It was, I realized, what people wore on their feet. It was a shoe toy.

"Oh, well, that's as good as it's going to get." CJ sighed. She turned around and gasped.

"Oh, Molly, no!"

I looked up and wagged when I heard my name. Very unfairly, CJ reached down when my attention was diverted and snatched my new chew toy away from me.

"Molly, this is . . . this is . . . oh boy." CJ sighed. "*Not a toy*, Molly. Okay?"

I wagged some more, waiting for her to give me the toy back. Instead, CJ yanked open the door where I'd seen the dog-that-was-not-a-dog and stood in front of it, hesitating.

I came to her side. There were lots of clothes in there, and that heavy, flowery scent wafted out. On the floor were many, many shoes. They all smelled as good as the one CJ now held in her hand, but with Gloria's smell so strong, I did not get the feeling they were for me. I looked up at CJ.

"You know what, Molly?" CJ said, staring into the closet. "I don't think she's going to miss it."

She handed me the shoe toy back, and I carried it happily out into the living room. I didn't really like that other room anyway. The dog-that-was-not-a-dog might come back.

I got to sleep with CJ again that night, and that was *wonderful.* In the morning, CJ cooked toast, and I got some. Then she scooped ice cream into a bowl, and I got some of that, too.

"Toast and ice cream . . . it's like cereal and milk. Right, Molly?" CJ asked me.

I wagged and licked the bowl perfectly clean.

When CJ took me out into the yard, everything was moist and the smells were deliciously strong. I squatted again and then dug up a few worms, but I didn't eat any. After you've done that a few times, you learn they're never going to taste any better than they smell.

We went back inside, and CJ washed up the dishes. Then she took me back to the park. Rocky did not show up with Trent this time, and I was disappointed. But another dog did. His name was Get Back Here Milo.

As soon as his owner snapped off his leash, Get Back Here Milo raced over to me. Since he was bigger and older, I knew what to do. I lay down on my back and showed him my belly, so he'd know that I understood the way things should be between us. He nosed me roughly, and then his owner called, "Get Back Here Milo!" and CJ picked me up, so he ran off again.

CJ sat down in the grass and set me down. Then she stretched out so that her face was near mine. I was so happy I yipped and spun. "She's coming back this afternoon," CJ said to me. "Can you go without barking tonight?"

I found a stick. I chewed until bits of bark came off in my mouth.

"I don't know what I'm going to do, Molly. She'll never let me keep you." CJ grabbed me and gave me a fierce hug, squeezing me a little harder than I actually liked. "I love you so much."

I could feel the affection pouring off her, and it made up for the way she was holding me. But I was really focused on the stick at the moment, so I didn't do much more than wag my tail.

When we got back home, I was very disappointed. CJ

took me straight from the yard to the basement and plopped me underneath the stairs again! I thought my girl had finally learned that everything was much better when we were together. I barked to let her know she'd made a mistake.

She understood. Instantly, the box slid back.

"I need you not to bark, okay, Molly?" my girl said. "She texted me from the airport. She'll be home any minute."

She slid the boxes back. I stared at them with disappointment, but the truth is, I was pretty tired from all the playing in the park. My new toy was in this small space for me, but I didn't even have the energy for a good chew right then. I curled up for a nap.

I'd bark for my girl later. She'd come.

I didn't think I'd been sleeping very long when a door slammed upstairs, waking me. "I'm home!" Gloria's voice boomed out. "Wait till you see what I bought in Aspen!"

5

Though I could always smell Gloria's scent anywhere in the house, I hadn't seen her for a while. Probably she'd be glad to see me now, just like CJ always was. I yipped a couple of times and waited, but all I heard was talking. I barked some more, and then I heard what I was expecting—the sound of footsteps on the stairs.

CJ shoved the boxes aside.

"Please, Molly, *please*. Please be quiet."

She had a bowl of food for me, and I gobbled it up. Then she tucked me inside her jacket and took me out the door that led straight to the backyard. I thought we were going to play in the grass, but instead she hurried out through a gate and along the sidewalk to the corner.

Then she let me down, and immediately I squatted in the grass and left my mark there. CJ patted and praised me. But her voice did not sound happy.

She took me back to the basement and into the small space. I tried to slip out as she pushed the boxes back in place, but I wasn't fast enough. Her feet ran up the stairs.

Then it was quiet.

I slept a little, but then I woke up and remembered I was all by myself. CJ had forgotten to come and get me so that we could sleep side by side.

I whimpered.

Upstairs, CJ was probably lying in her bed, feeling lonely because I wasn't with her. It was such a sad thought that I whimpered more loudly. Then I barked. And I barked some more.

"Clarity! What's that sound?" Gloria shrieked from overhead.

The basement door at the top of the stairs banged open.

"I think it came from down here!" CJ shouted. I wagged my tail happily as she came down the stairs. She'd heard me barking! She'd remembered how to play this game!

"Go back to bed, Gloria. I'll take care of it!" CJ called.

I heard CJ moving around on the other side of the boxes. I scratched at them, impatient for her to let me out. Our game had gone on long enough. I barked.

"There it is again!" Gloria said, panic in her voice. I could tell she was standing at the top of the stairs. "It's a dog! There's a *dog* in the house!"

At last, CJ shoved the boxes aside. I tumbled out, leaping into her arms, licking her face. "No, there's no dog!" she shouted. "It's . . . it's a fox! Stay back!"

"A *fox*? What? Are you sure?"

"Of course I'm sure! Foxes bark, you know!"

"How did it get into the house?" Gloria demanded from the top of the stairs. "What's a fox doing here?"

"Um, I bet the basement door blew open in the wind," CJ said quickly. "I bet it came in because it smelled your stupid coat!"

CJ smiled at me very quickly, and knelt down to put me on the floor. She stroked me, and I pressed close to her knees, wiggling a little with happiness to be next to my girl at last.

"That can't be right," Gloria said doubtfully. "Are you *sure* it's a fox?"

"I know what a fox looks like!" CJ called out, covering her smile with her hands. "It's a little one. I'm going to try to shoo it outside. Stay back! What if it runs up the stairs?"

I heard Gloria gasp and take a few steps backward.

CJ picked me up and ran with me out the basement door and into the yard.

Just like the last time, she didn't set me down. Instead,

she kept running, holding me tightly, until we'd gone down the sidewalk and turned the corner. Then she stopped and let me down on some new grass.

I stuck my nose into clump after clump of grass. There was a familiar smell everywhere I sniffed. Rocky had been here!

CJ knocked on a window. After a moment, the window opened and a head stuck out. I heard a bark from inside and barked back happily, greeting my brother.

"CJ? What are you doing here?" Trent asked sleepily.

"Take Molly!" CJ said, scooping me up. In a moment, I'd passed from her hands to his.

"Huh? What? Why are you giving me Molly?" Trent asked.

"Just keep her for tonight," CJ gasped. "I'll explain later. I really need this, Trent!"

"Well, okay." Trent pulled me in through the window and hugged me close to his chest. "But what's—"

"Thanks!" CJ gasped, and she took off running while Trent gaped and I squirmed and wiggled, trying to get free of his hands and outside to run with my girl. But Trent plopped me on the floor and shut the window, and then Rocky barreled into me, so excited to see me that he knocked me off my feet. By the time I shook him off and got my paws up on the windowsill, CJ was gone.

I whimpered. Trent sat down beside me and patted me. Rocky chewed on one of my back legs a little, so I had to get down and chase him around Trent's bedroom. After wrestling with my brother, I was so tired that I fell asleep in a lump on the carpet, even though Rocky was nibbling on my face.

When I woke up, CJ *still* wasn't there.

Rocky was sleeping next to me, though, so it was easy to pounce on him and start the day off with some wrestling. He was a little bigger than I was, but he usually let me pin him down when I wanted to.

"You two," Trent groaned from the bed. "It's not even five o'clock yet!"

Rocky stopped playing and ran over to the bed. Trent's hand was sticking out from under the covers, so Rocky nosed his way under it for some petting.

It made me miss CJ. Where was my girl? When was she coming to get me? I barked by the window a little so that she would hear me and know I was waiting for her.

"Aw, Molly," Trent said. He threw off the covers and came to sit by me, rubbing behind my ears. I leaned my head into his hand. He wasn't my girl, but he did know how to scratch just right. "You miss her, huh? I know how you feel."

After Trent had fed me and taken Rocky and me out to the backyard, the gate clanged open, and there she was. My girl!

I threw myself at her, and she scooped me up. Rocky jumped up and down by her feet as well, and I even growled at him a little bit for acting as if he were as important to CJ as I was.

CJ had a backpack on her back. She kissed me on top of my head, and she and Trent stood together, talking in hushed voices as Rocky ran in circles.

"What did you tell her?" Trent asked.

"That I had to leave early for school. Special project."

"*Are* you going to school?"

"Not today."

"CJ, you can't keep skipping school."

"Molly needs me."

"Yeah, but—"

"Thanks for taking care of her," CJ said, and she carried me out of the yard.

CJ and I played in the park for a while, and then she took me home. I was a little worried that I'd be back in the space under the stairs; I was getting really tired of that game. But CJ just stretched out on the living room couch with me, and held me while I took a nap.

When I woke up, however, CJ started that same old game up again.

She carried me down the stairs and tucked me into the small space. I tried to dart out and almost made it, but she slid the box back into place too quickly.

I sat down, frustrated. Why did my girl keep doing this?

I was puzzled by something else as well. CJ didn't go

up the basement stairs. She didn't go out the door into the backyard, either. She stayed on the other side of the boxes.

I barked to tell her to let me out.

"No!" CJ said harshly.

I jumped. My girl had never talked that way to me! I was so surprised that I just sat still, not sure what to do.

After a few minutes, CJ slid the box aside. "Good girl, Molly!" she said, and handed me a crunchy treat.

While I was happily eating it, she slid the box back into place. I barked.

"No!" CJ said.

And the game went on like that for a long, long time.

I didn't like being alone in the space under the stairs, and I could think of other games that were much more fun to play. What about Tug on a Towel? Or Chew on My New Toy? Or even just Lick the Girl Under the Chin?

But I came to understand that, if I stayed quietly under the stairs, I'd get a treat. If I barked, I'd get a "No!" from CJ.

I wasn't sure what to make of it all, or why the rules of the game had changed. But I played it, anyway. It wasn't as if there were anything else to do.

After we'd played Be Quiet for far too long, and had a few trips to the backyard for more fun, and had a nap or two, I heard a door upstairs open. "Okay, here she comes," CJ muttered. "Let's do this, Molly." She put me back under the stairs and slid the box into place.

I sat quietly.

CJ went up the stairs. I kept sitting. There were foot-steps on the ceiling above, and voices talking, and smells of food.

I kept sitting. Then I chewed on my toy. Then I waited some more.

It seemed to take forever, but at last CJ came down with praise and my treat, and let me out through the basement door for a long walk up and down several streets. I smelled a rabbit!

When we got back home, CJ put me back under the stairs, for *more* Be Quiet. I sighed and whimpered a little. But I was worn out from the long walk, and pretty soon I fell asleep.

I stirred awake when I heard footsteps coming down the basement stairs. They were heavier than my girl's, though, and that familiar flowery scent was coming down with them. I knew they belonged to Gloria.

She sighed and put something heavy down on the floor. "I hate laundry," she muttered. A metal door opened and, a few moments later, clanged shut.

"Gloria? What are you doing in the basement?" CJ's voice, sounding alarmed, came from the top of the stairs. A second later she was clattering down.

"What do you think?" Gloria's voice answered. "What else is there to do down here?"

I waited impatiently for CJ to let me out. I'd been quiet *forever*.

"Oh, sure, laundry. I forgot!" CJ said brightly and loudly. "Maybe I can help?"

I whined and scratched at the box, to remind CJ that I'd been extremely good and was ready for my treat.

"Well, sure," Gloria said, sounding a little baffled. "Get that stuff out of the washing machine, then."

"Okay! Got it!" CJ's voice was still loud. Maybe that's why she couldn't hear me whining. I tried again.

"Um, Gloria?"

"What is it?"

"I wanted to ask you. About. Um. About my dad?"

"What about him?" Gloria said shortly. "No, don't put that in the dryer. It's silk. It has to line dry."

"Okay, sure, got it. I mean, not about him so much. I mean, it's been a lot of years since the car accident. I don't think about him so much. Anymore."

"Five years," Gloria said. "Five years of being a single parent."

"Yeah, sure. I mean . . . I was thinking about . . . didn't he have relatives?"

"What relatives?" Gloria demanded.

"Well, I kind of remember. Wasn't there a farm? I think I was there, once at least. And a pond? A horse, maybe? Are they still there?"

"I wouldn't be surprised," Gloria said, sounding not much interested. "Your dad's mom wouldn't give that place up for a million dollars. I can't figure out why. A filthy barn with a horse in it, and that smelly pond, and a disgusting dog running around everywhere, even in the house. Why anybody would want to live like that . . ."

This game of Be Quiet was going on too long. I sighed with frustration and scratched louder at the boxes. Surely my girl hadn't forgotten the new rules?

"So, I was thinking," CJ said nervously. "Maybe I could visit one day? It's my grandmother who has the farm, right? I mean, I'd just like to—"

Something heavy thumped down on a metal surface.

"Certainly not," Gloria said. "I can't believe you'd ask that, Clarity."

"But I just want to know—"

"They treated me horribly. Horribly! You know this."

"Well, I know you didn't get along with them all the time, but—"

"They tried to tell me I didn't know how to take care of my own daughter!" Gloria sounded indignant. "How can you even think of this, Clarity? It's like you have no loyalty at all."

"I didn't mean it like that. I just wondered, that's all."

"Well, you can stop wondering. And bring those dry clothes up." Gloria marched up the stairs. A few seconds later, the box that shut me in slid aside and CJ was there, digging a treat out of her pocket for me.

"That was a close one, Molly!" she whispered. "Oh, girl . . . you're a good dog. Good, Molly." She fed me an extra treat and scooped me up to her face. I licked salty tears from her cheeks.

Then CJ told me to Be Quiet—again!—and pushed me back under the stairs, which was extremely unfair. I heard her go up the stairs. But she was back down very quickly with another treat, and took me out into the yard for a long time before bringing me back to the basement to sleep.

In the morning I was quiet some more, and then CJ came down with her backpack on to give me my treat and pet me and kiss me and take me out to the backyard. She was nervous, though; I could hear it in her voice and feel it in her hands as she petted me. "I'm sorry, Molly. I can't miss any more school," she whispered. "I have to go. I'll come back at lunchtime and let you out, okay?" She put me under the stairs. "Be good. *Be quiet.*"

In a hurry, she slid the box into place and dashed out into the backyard. Without me.

I sighed. I napped for a bit. I chewed on my toy, finally tearing it into two pieces. I wished I could show CJ what a good job I'd done.

Then I napped a bit more. There was nothing else to do. When I woke, I heard Gloria moving around upstairs.

Did Gloria know I was supposed to be fed treats for playing Be Quiet?

When I scratched at the box a little bit, I saw that CJ had not pushed it quite as far as she usually did. I scratched harder, and then I put my nose to the crack between the edge of the staircase and the surface of the box. I pushed. The box shifted just a little bit.

I pushed and scratched some more. Since I wasn't barking, this seemed okay to do. CJ had never said "No!" to pushing.

The crack got bigger and bigger. One last shove, and I could get my head through. Then my body followed, and I was out in the basement.

The basement wasn't much fun without CJ. The up-stairs always smelled more interesting. That's where the food was, and where the people spent most of their time, so the carpet and furniture all smelled like them.

I headed up the stairs.

It was hard work. I had to get my front paws on each step, and then heave and scramble to make my back paws climb up and meet them. But I kept going.

I could see that the door at the top of the stairs had been left open. Now there was only one step left. I got my front paws up, dug my claws into the floor, hauled my back legs up as well, and I was in the kitchen at last.

The doorbell rang. I licked up a spot of something

sticky and sweet on the floor, listening to Gloria walk through the living room and open the door.

"Yes?" she said.

I finished cleaning the floor, I shook myself, trotted toward Gloria's voice. Maybe she'd just forgotten about the treat. I'd be glad to remind her.

She was standing in the doorway. I headed across the living room floor to greet her. Air flowing through the open door was full of the fresh scent of grasses and trees and damp earth and all of the small nighttime animals who'd wandered across the yard while it was dark.

Someone else was standing at the door, right in front of Gloria. "Miss Mahoney?" she said. "I'm Officer Llewellyn. I'm a truant officer."

I trotted over to say hello to Gloria and to this new person. The woman on the porch glanced over Gloria's shoulder at me and then returned to the conversation.

"Truant officer? What are you talking about?" Gloria asked.

"I need to talk to you," the stranger said. "Your daughter has been absent from school too many times this semester."

Gloria just stood there, doing nothing, even though I was right by her side, waiting for my treat. I put a paw on her leg.

She looked down at me and screamed.

6

Gloria jumped out onto the porch, and I followed. I wagged my tail at her and the other woman standing there.

"That's not a fox!" Gloria yelped.

The new woman bent down and petted me. She had warm, gentle hands that smelled of soap and also of salty nuts. I licked them happily. "A fox?" she said, confused. "Of course it's not. It's a puppy."

"What's it doing in my house?" Gloria gasped.

The woman stood up. "I can't answer that, ma'am. It's *your* house. Here's a copy of the citation, along with a notice to appear." She handed Gloria some papers. "You'll need to come to court with your daughter. Understand?"

"What about the dog?"

I looked up at Gloria and wagged harder at the word "dog." Maybe she had finally remembered about my treat.

"What about it?"

"Take it with you!" Gloria demanded.

"I can't do that, ma'am."

"So you mean to tell me you're more concerned about a kid skipping a couple of classes than you are about a woman trapped on her own porch by a dog?"

"That's . . ." The new woman sounded bewildered. "That's right, yes."

"That's the stupidest thing I ever heard of!" Gloria cried out. "What kind of police officer are you?"

"I'm a truant officer, Miss Mahoney. I think you have everything you need now." The woman turned and walked off the porch.

"What do I do about the dog?" Gloria yelled after her.

"Call Animal Control, ma'am; that's what they do."

"All right, I will," Gloria muttered. She took a step sideways to where a broom was leaning against the wall of the house, and dropped the papers she was holding to grab it. She jabbed the bristly end at me.

I jumped back, and then leaped forward again, trying to catch the bristles in my teeth. This was a wonderful game!

"No!" Gloria shouted, real fear in her voice.

I stopped and looked up at her, tilting my head. I knew that word "no." But what was it about? Didn't she like the game? We could play something else if she wanted.

In one quick movement, Gloria stepped inside and slammed the door shut.

I stood for a few minutes, looking at the door, but it did not open up again. So I wandered down into the yard.

It was another nice day. Maybe that rabbit would be out looking for me. I left the yard and trotted down the sidewalk, sniffing at the bushes. It would be more fun to be outside with CJ, of course. Or Rocky to play and wrestle with. But still, this was better than playing Be Quiet under the stairs.

The air was rich with the fresh, juicy scents of leaves and grass, and sweet with flowers. I could smell where other dogs had left their marks on bushes and signposts, and where cats had rubbed against tree trunks and fences. Squirrels had darted across the grass, and I caught a whiff of the rabbit and followed it to a hole under a porch. When a car whizzed by, it added its own metallic, oily smell. My nose never stopped moving.

It was pretty clear that the rabbit wasn't going to come back out, so after I'd sniffed at its hole for a while, I kept moving. A trash can on a corner drew me close. There was food in there! It seemed like forever since CJ had brought me a bowl of crunchy things to eat.

Just by sniffing, I could tell that there were scraps of bread and bits of meat in the garbage, along with other things that smelled tasty, too. I stood up on my hind legs and stretched my front paws up as high on the can as they could go, but I couldn't reach anything. I dropped back down, and something crunched under my paws.

It was a thin, crinkly bag, and it smelled deliciously of salt. I stuck my nose deep inside it, licking hard. There were a few thin, crispy chips at the bottom, and I gobbled them up. The salt made me thirsty even as I ate, and burned my tongue like the ham had, but I couldn't stop.

Then I shook my head hard to get the bag off. It went flying. Across the street I spotted a squirrel, perched low on the trunk of a tree, near the ground. It looked excellent to chase. I needed to get over there!

But I paused at the edge of the curb and peered down at the street. So far I'd gone up steps, but never down. Up seemed easier. I put out a paw, hesitated, and then leaned farther over. Suddenly, I couldn't keep my balance any longer, and both front legs, followed by my head, came down onto the street. My back legs followed a second later.

I rolled over, got to my feet, and shook myself. A car came past, and I realized that I was closer to these giant, noisy, strange-smelling beasts than I had been while I was on the sidewalk.

Across the street, the squirrel scrambled a foot up the trunk. It was getting away! I barked and bunched my back legs under me, ready to sprint.

Then a big human hand came under my belly and scooped me up.

"Hey, there, little pup," a deep voice said. "That doesn't look safe."

I squirmed around to get a look at whoever had picked me up.

It was a big man with a rumbly voice and a fuzz of black hair on his face. In one hand—the one that wasn't holding on to me—he had a pole with a loop of shiny rope at the end. But he leaned that against a van that was parked by the curb and used his free hand to rub my ears.

He smelled interesting, of other dogs and soap, and there was something fresh and minty in his mouth. But right now I wanted that squirrel. I scrabbled with my paws to let him know to put me down.

"Calm down, now," he said, and he opened up the back door of the van. There was a strange-looking box in there, made all of metal wire. And a smell wafted out from it that I did not like. It smelled like fear, like more than one dog had been here and had been very, very afraid.

With one hand, the man opened up the door of the box. Deftly, he plopped me inside.

Then, as quickly as CJ would slide the boxes to trap me under the stairs, he shut the door.

I was stuck! I turned in a circle, bewildered. Lots of

other dogs had been in this box before me. I could tell. And most of them had been unhappy and frightened.

How was I going to get that squirrel now? When would CJ let me out?

"Hey!" a voice shouted.

The man turned at the sound of footsteps getting closer.

"Hey!" The second shout was louder. And I knew the voice.

It was CJ!

I put my paws up on the cage and barked with happiness. Somehow I knew we weren't playing Be Quiet now. And my girl was here! My tail beat the air.

"What are you doing?" CJ gasped, running up to the man who'd put me in here. She looked wide-eyed and frightened. "That's my dog!"

"Now wait," the man said. "Just wait."

"You can't take my dog!" CJ cried.

I began to get worried. CJ's voice was high-pitched and anxious, like that of a puppy who can't find her mother. I could tell she needed me. Why didn't she just let me out and pick me up?

"We had a complaint," the man told CJ. "And this dog was running around loose."

I yipped to remind CJ that I was here, and waiting.

"Complaints? Molly's just a puppy," CJ said. "Who complains about a puppy?"

I yipped louder at hearing my name.

The man shook his head. "She's got no collar. No tag. Nothing to say where she belongs."

"She belongs with me!" CJ said frantically. "Can't you tell? Look at her!"

I tried chewing on the wire, but it hurt my teeth. So I just jumped up as high as I could reach and barked and squirmed and did everything I could to tell my girl to come and get me.

"Listen, hon," the man said. "If she's your dog, you can pick her up at the shelter anytime after noon tomorrow."

"But wait! Wait!" Tears were flowing down CJ's face now. I whimpered, wanting to kiss her sadness away. Why wouldn't she pick me up so I could take care of her? "She won't understand if you take her away. She'll think I don't care about her. Please, please. I don't know how she got out, but I promise you it won't happen again. Promise, promise. Please?"

The man took in a deep breath and let it out slowly. "Well . . . all right, look. Okay. But you need to get her a collar and a tag. And take her to the vet. Get her vaccinated, get her a microchip, and in a few months, spay her. And then get a license. It's the law."

CJ gasped and blotted at her tears. "I will. I really will. Please, please, can I have my dog?"

The man reached in and opened up the door of the metal box.

I bounded out into CJ's arms. I didn't get a treat this time—maybe I hadn't been quiet enough. But I didn't care. It was enough to be close to CJ, to lick at her salty tears, and wag my tail hard against her body.

"Thank you," CJ whispered. "Thank you."

"All right," the man said. "But keep your promise."

CJ nodded frantically, still holding me tightly. The man got into the van and drove away.

CJ held me tightly. "Oh, Molly," she whispered. "Oh, Molly, I guess we'd better go home."

I could feel her heart beating hard in her chest, and it didn't quiet down as we walked back to the house. It thudded as we walked up the porch steps. CJ glanced down at the papers that were still scattered across the boards of the porch, bent to pick one up, and looked at it.

She stood there for a little while, holding me close, with that paper in her hand. Then she opened the door and stepped inside.

"Clarity? Is that you?"

Gloria came into the living room from the kitchen and then stopped, staring at me. Staring at CJ and me, together.

I wagged. I was willing to go over to Gloria and say hello, but CJ held me tightly. In fact, it was a little uncomfortable, but I was willing to put up with that to be next to my girl.

"What is that?" Gloria demanded.

"This is Molly. She's my dog."

It wasn't just CJ's heart beating hard now. She was shaking all over. I burrowed my head under her chin, trying to get as close to her as possible, to let her know I would always be there to look after her.

"No. It is *not*," Gloria said. "Out! Take it out of here!"

"No!" CJ jerked her chin up.

"You cannot have a dog in my house!"

"I'm keeping her!"

"You can't make any demands like that just now. Do you know what trouble you're in? A truant officer came to my door! You've been missing so much school they came out here to arrest you!"

CJ set me down. I sat on her feet.

"Did you even bother to read this?" CJ asked. She waved the paper at Gloria. "It doesn't say anything about arresting me. But it does say you have to come to court with me."

"Well. Well!" Gloria stood up straighter and stared down at CJ. "And I will tell them you are completely out of control."

"And I'll tell them why!"

I could tell that CJ was more angry than frightened now. Her voice said it, and so did her hands, tightened into fists by her sides.

"What do you mean, why?"

"Why I was able to skip so much school! You go on

trips all the time and leave me here. Without any adults. What do you think a judge in court will think about that?"

"I don't believe this. You *asked* to be left alone. You hated the babysitter I found for you!"

"I don't think a judge will care about that," CJ said firmly, and I could tell that Gloria was the one who was anxious now. I looked around nervously to see what the threat was, but all I saw was the living room—couch, fireplace, coffee table, bookshelf. It looked the same as always.

"Unless," CJ said in a low voice. "Unless you let me keep Molly."

I heard my name. I looked up at my girl's face.

"What on earth?" Gloria demanded.

"If you let me keep Molly, I won't tell anybody about your little trips," CJ told her. "Not the judge. Not the principal. Not anybody. I'll say I told you I was going to school, but I was actually skipping. I'll say it wasn't your fault."

"It *wasn't* my fault!" Gloria said indignantly.

"And Molly will help keep me safe," CJ added. "When you go away. *Again*. If I have Molly, I won't mind. I'll never tell anybody, no matter how long you stay away for."

"A dog? In my house? I can't believe this, Clarity. You know how I feel about dogs."

"And you know how I feel about Molly. So what do you want me to do?"

Gloria threw out her hands, one to each side. "Fine. Fine! But I'm not doing a bit of work to look after that thing."

She turned around and walked back into the kitchen.

CJ let out her breath in a long, shaking sigh. She sat down and pulled me onto her lap. I was happy to get on with the business of kissing her chin and letting her pet me from nose to tail.

"Oh, Molly," CJ whispered. "I guess we won."

That night I got to cuddle in my girl's bed again. I was so excited that of course I had trouble sleeping, but CJ put her hand on me and petted me slowly and gently until I got drowsy. I leaned against her and felt my love flowing into her, and hers flowing into me.

I woke up later because I could hear someone walking down the hall. Gloria.

The door from CJ's bedroom to the hallway was open a little. Gloria pushed it open a bit more. Then she stood there, staring in at me on the bed.

I wagged. Just a little. I did not want to wake up my girl.

Gloria didn't seem happy to see either of us. She just stared at me from the darkened hallway.

7

After that day, CJ and I never played Be Quiet under the stairs again. I was very glad about that.

Most days, CJ did go away for much longer than I thought necessary. She would put her backpack on in the mornings after she'd fed me and herself, and she'd bend down to pet me and kiss me on my head. "I have to go to school, Molly," she'd say. It got so that I'd whimper a little when I heard the word "school." I knew it meant my girl would be leaving me.

I usually stayed in CJ's room while she was gone, since her smell was strongest there. But Gloria would let me out into the backyard whenever I needed to go there. And in the afternoon, CJ would be back again, to scoop me up and cuddle me and take me to the park or in the yard for a good long run and lots of playing.

Some days she didn't do school, and then we could be together all the time. Sometimes we stayed home, but more often we visited friends. I loved it best when we went to see Trent and Rocky. CJ must have liked that best, too, because we went there more than any other place.

It was good to get a chance to play with my brother. Rocky and I would tear around Trent's backyard or inside in his room, wrestling until we both collapsed with exhaustion. Then I'd lie on top of him for a while, holding his leg in my mouth out of sheer affection.

CJ was happier at Trent and Rocky's house than she was at home with Gloria. I could tell. She smiled more often and laughed more loudly, and her body was more relaxed as she sat on the floor of Trent's room. It made me so happy that sometimes I'd have to leave Rocky and run over to fling myself on her lap and roll over so that she could rub my belly.

"You think maybe she's a schnauzer-poodle?" CJ asked Trent one day as she rubbed. "A schnoodle?"

"I don't think so," Trent answered. He was sitting on the floor a little ways from CJ, playing Tug on a Sock with Rocky. "Maybe a Doberman-poodle."

"A doodle?"

I liked the sound of that word. I wagged harder.

"Or a spaniel of some kind," Trent said.

"Molly, you could be a schnoodle, a spoodle, or a doodle, but you're not a poodle," CJ said, holding me close and kissing my nose. I wagged harder.

"Hey, watch this," Trent told CJ. "Rocky!" Rocky sat up straight and looked right at his boy. "Sit! Sit!" Trent said. Rocky lowered his rear end to the ground, his eyes on Trent the whole time.

I watched my brother, baffled. What had happened to our excellent game of I'm Faster Than You Are?

"Good dog!" Trent said, and Rocky jumped up. I figured our game was back on and chased him under the bed.

"I'm not teaching Molly any tricks," CJ said. "I get enough orders in my life."

"Are you kidding?" I heard Trent say as I stuck my nose under the bed and got ahold of Rocky's dusty tail. "Dogs want to work. I got this book; that's what it said. Watch. He likes it. Rocky!"

Rocky squirmed out from under the bed, twitched his tail out of my mouth, and gave his attention back to Trent.

"Sit!" Trent said again. Rocky sat.

Anything my brother did, I could do. I put my rear end on the floor, too, and waited for somebody to tell me I was a good dog.

"Look, Molly figured it out by watching Rocky! You're

such a good dog, Molly!" Trent exclaimed. "You, too, Rocky. Good dog!"

Rocky and I both wagged for being good dogs. Then Rocky rolled over for a belly rub, so I put my teeth on his throat.

"Hey, so . . ." Trent said.

Rocky froze and then wiggled out of my grip. I'd felt it, too—a sudden whiff of fear from Trent. I looked up alertly. Rocky pushed his muzzle under Trent's hand, while I checked on CJ.

She was sitting on the floor, leaning back against Trent's bed. Whatever Trent was afraid of, it wasn't bothering her.

"There's that dance at school. You know?"

"Saw the posters," CJ said. She didn't sound interested.

"Maybe . . . I don't know . . . do you want to go?"

"Nah. Who'd ask me?" CJ laughed.

Trent's face was growing red. Rocky wiggled his whole body under his boy's hand to see if that would help.

"Well, I just did," he said, not very loudly.

"What? No, are you kidding? You don't go to a dance with your *friends*," CJ said, laughing. "That's not what it's for."

Trent picked up Rocky and held him close to his face. "Yeah, but . . . ," he mumbled into my brother's fur.

"But what? You go with a girlfriend, that's what you do. Ask somebody pretty. What about Susan? I know she likes you."

"No, I'm . . ." Trent put Rocky down in his lap. "Pretty? CJ, come on. You know you're pretty."

"Goof." CJ laughed again. "Okay, show me what else you've taught Rocky."

Trent was frowning and looking at the ground. "I haven't taught him anything else," he said.

CJ stared at him. "What's wrong?"

"Nothing. So what's up with the truant stuff?" he asked CJ.

Now Trent wasn't scared anymore, but he wasn't happy, either. I knew he'd be better soon, though, since Rocky was with him. I flopped down next to CJ and rolled onto my back, presenting my belly to be rubbed.

CJ scratched. I wiggled with pleasure.

"Oh, it's such a pain," she said. "I've got detention, but it's not like regular detention. It's this weirdo kind of art class instead."

"Seriously? You skip school and get to go to art?"

"Yeah, bizarre, huh? It's after school, and it starts next week. But I can't miss a day. Not one! If I do, no more art class, and they pull me out of regular classes, too. I have to sit in some room with a computer and learn all by myself."

"Well, I hate to say I told you so, but—"

"So don't!" CJ jumped up. "Let's take the dogs for a walk."

Walk! I knew that word! It was a *wonderful* word! Rocky and I both tore around Trent's room in a frenzy of happiness.

A few days later, CJ took me on another walk right after she got home from school. I was glad, but for some reason CJ seemed in a hurry. Normally, she was very nice about letting me sniff for as long as I wanted, unless I found something deliciously dead. Then she always pulled me away. I never understood why.

But this time she walked briskly, and I only got whiffs of other dogs and squirrels and mouthwatering pieces of trash from the tufts of grass as we passed.

"Come on, Molly. We can't be late!" CJ insisted.

I didn't understand why we were in such a rush, but at least she was taking me with her. "There's the art building," she said, and she broke into a quick jog. I stayed close at her side.

She pushed open a door, and smells wafted out at me. Some were sharp and made my eyes sting. Some were chalky and dusty. Some were rich and almost seemed like something to eat—but not quite. Some smelled like the dirt in the yard after it had rained.

I stood still, my nose working as hard as it could to sort out all the new smells as CJ talked to a tall woman who came to greet her.

"Um, it's all right to bring my dog, right?" CJ said. She was nervous. I pressed close to her leg. "I called and asked. I talked to someone in the office and she said okay, as long as she behaves. She's really good."

"I'm sure she is," the woman said. "Hi, CJ. I'm Sheryl. Welcome. Why don't you take a seat? We'll get started in a minute."

CJ sat down at a table and took off her jacket, tossing it over another chair. I stayed by her side a bit and then wandered off to explore.

There was a sink, and another doorway that led (I could tell by sniffing underneath the closed door) into a hallway. There was a desk where Sheryl was pulling open drawers to find something. And there were a lot of tables. Kids were sitting at each one. "Aw, cute dog!" one of them said, and soon hands were coming out from all directions to pet me. I licked a lot of fingers and even lapped at a few faces that came down close to mine.

I thought CJ and I would probably like the art building just fine.

After that, we did art building three times a week. CJ would sit at a table and draw, or stand at an easel and smear paints on its surface. I liked the smell of the paints, but not of the turpentine she'd used to clean her hands afterward. I wouldn't let her pet me until the smell had worn off a little.

That was all right, though, because there were plenty

of other kids there who wanted to stroke my back or rub behind my ears. "Hi, Molly!" they'd call. "CJ, I brought a treat for Molly. Can I give it to her?" "Hey, Molly, come here!" I loved hearing so many different voices call my name. I'd wander among the tables while CJ worked with her paints and pencils, and I'd collect all the attention I could.

There was one boy who never petted me, though, even though he sat at CJ's table. He looked at CJ a lot. I noticed that, because I looked at her a lot, too. But the way he did it seemed different from the way I did. I looked at her because she was my girl, and I needed to be alert to everything she did. He looked at her as if he were angry with her, even if she was just sitting quietly, rubbing a pencil on a sheet of paper.

I heard Sheryl call his name often. "Shane, can you get started, please?" she'd say. "Shane, show me your progress. Shane, keep your attention on your own work."

I didn't mind that Shane never petted me, because I didn't like the way he smelled. Sometimes there was a sour, smoky odor on his hands and breath. But even when that scent wasn't there, he smelled of anger and frustration and, way underneath, of fear.

Dogs who are frightened are usually the ones who snap at you for no reason, even if you're just trying to play a fun game of It's My Ball and You Can't Have It. I tried to stay away from Shane.

One time, right after we got to the art building, Sheryl called CJ up to the front of the room. Of course I went with her. "Up here," Sheryl said, smiling.

CJ lifted me up to the top of Sheryl's desk. There was a bright red pillow there, and a soft, dark green blanket. CJ plopped me down on the blanket.

"Perfect!" Sheryl said, reaching out to pet me. I licked her. Her fingers tasted like clay. "Look how her black fur just glows against those colors. Will she stay there, do you think?"

"I think so," CJ said. "If I sit nearby."

"Good. Then you sit at this end of the desk. Everyone else ready? I can't wait to see the Molly portraits you're going to come up with!"

CJ settled down in a chair close by me. "Stay there, Molly," she said to me.

I wagged to hear my name. Then I peered over the edge of the desk. It seemed like a long way down, and even though I wanted to walk around the tables and get petted by all my new friends, I didn't feel like jumping.

Besides, the pillow was very soft, and the blanket was cozy, and CJ was nearby. I curled up contentedly, tucking my tail under my nose.

"Perfect," Sheryl said softly from behind me. "Okay, everyone, paint!"

The room got very quiet. There was just the sound of brushes licking across paper. It was soothing. I began to

drift into a half-asleep, half-awake state. If CJ said anything I'd perk right up, but for right now a snooze seemed
best.

"You brought in a dog?" I heard a man's voice say.

I twitched one ear but didn't bother to sit up. The
voice was coming from far away, in the doorway that connected the art room to the hallway.

Sheryl's voice, from the same place, answered it.
"That's Molly. She comes every week."

"Are you sure that's wise?"

"Nobody's allergic. I checked. And everybody loves
her." Sheryl laughed a little. "Honestly, nobody's missed
a day this semester, and I think it's because of Molly."

The man's voice chuckled. "Maybe we should have
dogs in the regular classrooms, too. Everything going
well? No problems?"

"None so far."

"How about . . ." The man's voice trailed off.

Sheryl lowered her voice, too, but I was still able to
hear easily. "Shane? I don't know. He comes to every
class, and he does the work—well, eventually. But it's
pretty clear he's only here because he has to be."

"That's true of a lot of them, though, isn't it?"

"Maybe the first few times. But most of them really
come to enjoy it. Shane, though . . . I'm not getting
through to him. Not the way I want to."

"But he's not causing trouble?"

"Nothing I can't handle," Sheryl said.

I could hear the man's footsteps going away down the hall. Sheryl walked among the tables. I opened one eye to check on CJ, who was bent over her paper, frowning with concentration. Then I closed both eyes and went to sleep for real, happy to be with my girl.

8

It was a shame I couldn't stay with my girl all day, every day. But whenever she was doing school, I was stuck at home with Gloria.

I tried to show Gloria that, even though CJ was my girl, I was perfectly willing to be friendly to her, too. But it was pretty clear that Gloria didn't want that. If I came close to ask for an ear scratch or a back rub, she'd push me away. If I stood near the back door to go out, she'd sigh with impatience before she opened it, and she often forgot to let me back in. I'd have to bark very loudly to remind her.

Somehow, I got the feeling that, around Gloria, I was never a good dog.

That's why I was so surprised when, one day while

CJ was doing school, Gloria actually talked to me when I came into the kitchen.

"There you are," she said.

Her voice was not very friendly. I kept my rear end lowered to show that I understood she was the boss, and I wagged a little, hoping she'd be happier if she knew I was no threat. She was standing near the refrigerator with the door open, holding something in her hand.

I came a little closer to see if it might be food.

"Yuck," Gloria said. She often said that when I was around, but I never could figure out what it meant. "Look at this cheese. I swear I just bought it."

She glanced from the thing she was holding to me, and then she closed the refrigerator door. Too bad. There were things in there that I would have liked to smell some more.

"Want a treat?" she asked.

My rear end came untucked, and my head lifted. Treat? I knew *that* word!

"A dog won't mind a little mold, I guess," Gloria said. She pulled some thin plastic away from the object in her hand, and an enticing, rich smell wafted out. Cheese! Saliva began to gather in my mouth.

She broke off a chunk of the cheese, jabbed a long metal fork into it, and held it out to me.

I sniffed at it hopefully. She held it still. I nibbled at

it tentatively and hesitated, waiting for her to get angry, to call me a bad dog.

"Go on, take it," Gloria said impatiently.

I pulled the cheese off the fork, dropped it to the floor, and ate in two gulps. Clearly, Gloria had decided that I was a good dog after all!

"Here," Gloria said. With a clang, she dropped the rest of the cheese in my bowl. How wonderful! CJ never gave me treats this big!

"Make yourself useful," Gloria said. "Ridiculous we spend so much on all that expensive dog food when you could just eat up stuff that's gone bad."

I picked up the heavy block of cheese and then dropped it back into the bowl. I honestly wasn't sure how to go about eating something this size. But when Gloria left the kitchen, I settled down to the serious work of gnawing one off one bite at a time.

By the time I'd gotten it all down, I was drooling a little and very thirsty. I lapped up most of my water.

Gloria came through the kitchen a few minutes later. "Finished?" she asked. "Okay, out!" She opened the door to the backyard and stood by it. I got the sense of what she wanted and hurried outside. It felt better out there, anyway. Gloria's voice and posture said I was still a bad dog, while the cheese said I was good. It was confusing. I was glad to lie in the grass and not think about it for a while.

The earth was cool against my belly, and the sun was

warm along my back. I wished I had some more water, but it was too much trouble to get up and bark at the back door for Gloria to let me in so I could go to my bowl. For now, I was content just to lie there and fall asleep.

When I woke up, I knew something was wrong.

I was thirstier than ever, which didn't make much sense, because my mouth was flooded with saliva. It was running out of my mouth and onto the grass. I shook my head, which made me dizzy, and I got up, but my legs were trembling so much it was hard to walk. All I could do was brace my legs far apart and stand there so that I wouldn't fall, waiting for my girl to come.

I don't know how long it took, but my girl *did* come. I heard her footsteps inside the house. Then the door banged open.

"Molly! Come! Come in!" CJ called.

I wanted to be with my girl. I knew I was supposed to be with my girl. I took a wobbly step, holding my head low.

"Molly?" CJ came out onto the grass. "Molly? Are you okay? *Molly?*"

The last time she said my name, it was a scream.

I wanted to go to her. I knew she was worried and afraid. It was my job to be near her, but I just couldn't budge.

When she came running to me and picked me up, I could hear her voice talking to me, but it sounded like my head was buried under the covers. Everything was muffled and quiet.

"Mom! There's something wrong with Molly!" CJ cried.

"I'm sure she'll be fine," Gloria's voice answered from somewhere inside the house.

"No! Mom! Come now! She has to go to the vet!"

My stomach heaved. CJ set me down. Vomit exploded out of my mouth and into the grass.

"What did you eat? What did you eat? Oh, Molly!" CJ cried out. "Mom, come now. You have to drive. Hurry up!"

"Stop yelling. All the neighbors will hear you!" Gloria appeared in the doorway as CJ scooped me up again. "All right. But if she throws up in my car . . ."

"Come on!" CJ shouted, running with me to the driveway.

My girl sat in the back with me, holding me on her lap. "We're going to the vet," she told me as the car started moving. "Okay? Molly? Are you okay? Molly, *please!*"

I knew that my girl needed something from me. I managed to lick her hand as it stroked my face. But it was getting dark in the car, darker and darker. I felt my tongue flop out of my mouth.

"Molly!" CJ shouted. "Molly!"

* * *

I opened my eyes slowly, blinking again and again. All I could see was a fuzzy light. I felt sleepy, my head too heavy to hold up, my legs floppy. Had I somehow become a puppy again?

I whined and squirmed a little, hoping to find my mother. But I couldn't smell her. I couldn't smell anything, really. I groaned, feeling myself begin to slide back into sleep.

"Molly?"

I jerked awake. It was CJ's voice! My girl was near me!

I blinked again and again, and my vision cleared. I could see CJ close beside me. She put her face next to mine.

"Oh, Molly, I was so worried about you." Her hands stroked my fur, and she kissed my face. I wagged, my tail beating softly on something metal. A table. I was in the vet's office, I realized. I still felt too weak to raise my head, but I could reach out to lick CJ's hand. Thank goodness I was still alive to take care of my girl.

I'd been to see the vet before, and I knew her name was Dr. Marty. I didn't like the way she smelled, but she did have good, gentle hands. She was standing behind CJ now, talking to her. "Her last seizure was very short, more than three hours ago. I think we're out of the woods."

"But what made her so sick?" CJ asked, her voice a little tearful.

"I don't know," Dr. Marty said. "She obviously got into something she shouldn't have."

"Oh, Molly," CJ said. "Don't eat bad things, okay?"

I licked her face as she kissed me again.

After a while I felt better, and could lift my head, and then stand. I lapped up some water eagerly, and CJ took me home.

Gloria sat in the front seat, driving. I could tell she was angry. The tension in her muscles and the way she held her head made it obvious. I huddled in CJ's lap in the backseat. It was hard to imagine how I'd been a bad dog, when I felt so weak. But Gloria made me feel that way.

CJ carried me inside and put me down on the soft cushions of the sofa.

"Not on the couch!" Gloria said.

CJ gave her an angry look, but she gently boosted me down to the floor and sat beside me.

Gloria stood looking down at both of us. "Six hundred dollars!" she said.

"Molly almost died!" CJ said back. Her voice was as angry as Gloria's.

Gloria threw out both hands in exasperation and walked down the hall to her room. Her door slammed.

CJ scooped me up and carried me to her bed, where she cuddled me until I fell asleep again.

It took me a few days to feel like myself. By the time

I did, it was one of those days when CJ did not have to do school. Gloria had gone out, so we were both able to sit on the couch. CJ was looking at the screen on the wall, which I had learned was called a "TV," and I was wondering why people liked to look at that thing so much. It didn't even smell interesting!

Then the doorbell rang. I hurried by CJ's side as she went to answer it. One of my jobs was to inspect people who came to the door. She opened it, and her voice sounded surprised.

"Oh, Shane."

"Hey," Shane's voice said.

"Hey," CJ said. "What's up?"

"Nothing," Shane said. "You want to hang out?"

"Um. Here?"

"Yeah. Why not?"

CJ hesitated, but then she opened the door all the way. I still didn't like Shane's smell. I barked once to let him know that this was my house and I'd protect everything here. Then I wagged.

"Okay, sure, I guess," CJ said. "We're just watching TV, me and Molly. You want to come in?"

Shane came in, and he and CJ sat down on the couch to do more staring at the TV. I sniffed Shane's shoes and jeans thoroughly, and he put his hand on my head and pushed me away.

"She's just trying to get to know you," CJ said.

"Yeah, whatever," Shane mumbled.

CJ scooped me up and put me on the couch between them. "Is this okay to watch?"

"I guess," Shane said. "Do you have anything to eat?"

"Sure." CJ got up, and I jumped down to the floor. "No, you just stay there," she told Shane. "I'll bring it out."

I followed CJ into the kitchen. She was happier there than she'd been in the living room, so I wagged a few times. We heard the volume of the TV go up in the other room.

CJ got a wonderfully crinkly bag out of the cupboard and poured some glasses full of something that fizzed. Then she carried all this back into the living room. She handed the bag to Shane, so I went and sat next to him.

I knew exactly what was in those bags. I watched his face carefully. Sooner or later, I knew, a chip would fall to the floor. It always did.

"So." Shane crunched. "That art class is a drag, huh?"

"I kind of like it," CJ said. She was twisting a shoe-lace around her finger.

Shane put another chip in his mouth. Couldn't he tell that I was sitting right here in front of him? Didn't he understand about sharing? The chips in the bag were for him. The ones that fell on the floor were for me. That was how CJ and I always did it.

"You're kidding." Shane snorted. Then the doorbell

rang again. It was hard to leave the chips to go with CJ, but it was my job, so I did it.

Before the door even opened, I knew it was Trent. My tail began to swish back and forth in a wide arc.

"Hey, how's Molly?" Trent asked as soon as CJ opened the door. "Molly girl! There you are!" He bent down to take my head in his hand and rub his fingers along my ears. I wiggled happily.

CJ was smiling. "She's better. See?"

"Hey, CJ, you coming back?" Shane yelled from the living room.

Trent straightened up. His grin faded.

"Who's that?"

"Somebody I know from art class," CJ said. "Come on in, Trent, we're just watching TV."

"Uh, no, my mom said I had to mow the lawn," Trent said. He shifted his weight from foot to foot. I leaned against his knees to remind him that my ears could use more attention.

"Can't you do it later?" CJ asked.

"No. She said now. I just wanted to check on Molly," Trent said.

"Come over later?" CJ asked.

Trent shrugged. "Glad Molly's okay," he said, and he hurried away down the front walk.

CJ went back into the living room slowly. She didn't

sit on the couch again. Instead, she settled down into a chair across the room. She and Shane looked at the TV for a while, until the bag of chips was empty. Then Shane left.

He didn't even feed me one chip.

9

The next day, after school, we did art building. I didn't get to sit on a table this time. That was all right, though. I walked through the room and got petted as much as I wanted, and then I settled down by CJ's easel.

She was frowning, rubbing paint onto a rectangle of canvas with a fierce look of concentration. But she was happy, too. I could just tell. I lay down close enough to her that I could reach over and touch her with my nose if I needed to, and I dozed for a while.

When I woke up, the students were splashing water in a sink and opening and closing doors. CJ, though, stayed right at her easel, even after the other kids all piled out of the door.

Shane went, too, his hands shoved into his pockets, his head lowered. He didn't talk to anybody.

Sheryl came over to talk to CJ. "How much longer do you think you'll need?" she asked.

"Maybe another hour?" CJ said. "Thanks for letting me stay late."

"Far be it from me to interrupt inspiration," Sheryl said. "But I do have to run down to the office and take care of some paperwork. Are you okay on your own? I'll be back to lock up."

"I'm fine," CJ said. "Anyway, I'm not on my own. Molly's with me."

Sheryl smiled. "See you in a little while, then. I'll just lock the outside door before I go."

CJ and I were alone in the art building.

I did a quick tour of the room, in case any of the students who'd left had dropped something interesting to eat. Then I settled down by CJ's side again.

"You're a good girl, Molly," she whispered. "Not too much longer, okay?"

Somebody knocked on the door that led outdoors. CJ jumped, and a brush fell on the floor with a splat.

I sniffed, but it wasn't edible. "No, Molly, don't lick that!" CJ said, snatching it up. She hurried to the door. I kept close by her.

CJ stared through the door's window. "Shane?" she asked.

The knocking came again. "Come on, CJ, open up!" Shane's voice called.

CJ twisted a latch that stuck out from the door's surface. Then she tugged at the knob and opened it, but not all the way. "What's going on?" she asked.

"Sheryl took my cell phone," Shane said from the other side of the door. "Hey, let me in, CJ. Don't be like that. She said she'd give it back to me at the end of class, but I guess she forgot. And I need it. I have to call my ride, or I'll just be standing out here all night. Come on."

CJ pulled the door open farther and took a step back. "I guess. Come in."

Shane stepped inside. I stayed near CJ. Her voice was tight, and she hugged her arms across her chest. I could tell she was nervous. This wasn't my house, so I didn't need to protect it from Shane, but I did need to protect my girl.

Shane hurried across the room to a big desk where Sheryl often sat or stood when she was talking to the children. He pulled open one drawer, then another, and stuffed something into his pocket.

"Got it!" he said.

"So, okay," CJ said. "Should I tell Sheryl you took your phone back, or . . . ?"

"Man, CJ, why would you do that?" Shane shook his head and laughed. "I thought you were cool. Just don't say anything, right? She doesn't like me. You'd probably get in trouble for letting me in. Hey, I'll come over another day, watch more TV or something. See you!" He hurried out of the door. CJ looked after him for a moment before she shut it and twisted the metal latch again.

She went back to her easel, but she wasn't as happy as she'd been before. She only painted a few more minutes before she carried the brushes to the sink and ran water over them. By the time Sheryl came back, she was ready to go.

The next day, after breakfast, CJ went out into the yard with me. She was throwing a ball, and I was chasing it when Gloria called out of the back door.

"CJ, some teacher's here to see you!"

I snatched up the ball in my mouth and followed CJ inside.

Sheryl was standing in the hallway. I bounded up to her, and she rubbed behind my ears, but not for very long. I was disappointed. I thought Sheryl understood about ear rubs.

She was frowning, but not in an angry way. More as if she were worried. Ear rubs would probably help with that.

"CJ, I need to talk to you about something," she said.

"Um." CJ looked worried, too. "Okay. Come in."

"Your mother should probably be present," Sheryl said, walking into the living room.

"Why?" Gloria came in from the kitchen and stood

stiffly by the door. "Is there some kind of problem? My daughter's gone to that art class every week. She hasn't missed a day. If the school is saying she hasn't—"

"No, it's nothing like that." Sheryl sat down. So did CJ. I brought the ball to my girl and nudged her hand with it, but she didn't throw it. I lay down on the floor by her feet with a sigh. People, not dogs, usually decide when games are over. I wished it could be the other way around.

"Did you let someone into the art room last night, CJ?" Sheryl asked.

CJ froze. I bounded back up. My girl was afraid! I pressed close to her side. She looked back and forth from Gloria to Sheryl. She opened her mouth and closed it again.

"I need you to tell the truth, CJ," Sheryl said. "Please don't try to protect anyone. This is serious."

"Protect?" Gloria sat up stiffly in her chair. "Who would she be protecting? What's the point of all these questions?"

"Could you just let CJ answer, please, Mrs. Mahoney?"

"It's *Miss*," Gloria said.

I put my head in CJ's lap and whined a little.

CJ put both hands on my head and smoothed back my ears. She bent low, close to my face. "You're a good girl, Molly. It's okay," she said.

Then she lifted her head and looked at Sheryl. "I let

Shane in. He said his phone was in your desk, and he needed it to call whoever was giving him a ride."

I could sense Sheryl relaxing. Her shoulders went down a little, and her hands settled quietly in her lap.

"What did Shane do after you let him in?" she asked quietly.

"He just got his phone out of your desk and left again," CJ answered.

Sheryl sighed softly. "No, I'm afraid he didn't, CJ. He took *my* phone out of my desk. And some money that I'd left there, too."

Fear spiked inside CJ, and her eyes opened wide.

"He did? But I didn't know! I didn't know he was going to do that! He just said he needed *his* phone. Sheryl, I really didn't know!"

"Is my daughter being accused of something?" Gloria demanded.

Sheryl shook her head. Her voice sounded sad.

"Miss Mahoney, I'm not accusing CJ of anything. But I'm afraid this doesn't look good for her. I'm going to explain to the principal about Shane, but he'll have to report the theft to the police. Hopefully we can get my phone back, and the money, too. That will help. And I'll tell the principal you told me the truth, CJ."

"I'm not a thief," CJ whispered.

Her eyes filled up with tears. I licked urgently at her

hands, wishing I could crawl up into her lap. I was sure that would make her feel better. But Gloria always said, "Bad dog!" if I got on the couch while she was in the room. I didn't want to be a bad dog now.

"I believe you, CJ. I do." Sheryl's voice was warm. "Try not to worry. I'm afraid Shane is likely to be expelled. This isn't the first problem he's had at the school. But hopefully that won't happen to CJ."

"Expelled?" CJ gasped.

"My daughter is certainly not going to be expelled!" Gloria said. "I'll talk to the principal myself. Clarity June, how could you have behaved like this? Do you realize what people will think?"

"I didn't know he'd take something!" CJ said, rubbing her eyes. I licked the salty tears helpfully off her hand.

Gloria's voice rose. "First you skip school. Now this! Really, Clarity. You make things impossible. Maybe you don't care about yourself, but do you realize how embarrassing this all is for me?"

Sheryl looked from CJ to Gloria, a small, puzzled frown on her face. CJ bent down and hugged me tightly. A little too tightly, actually, but I could sense she needed me, so I didn't try to wiggle away.

"There's no need to panic," Sheryl said quietly, getting up. "I'll tell the principal what CJ said to me and that she's been a good student in my class. Not to mention quite a talented artist." CJ looked up at that, and I felt her surprise. "The school will be in touch. Don't worry too much, CJ. It will work out, I'm sure."

Sheryl left. Usually, it was one of my jobs to walk people to the door, but this time it felt more important to stay close to CJ.

"Really, Clarity June," Gloria said after Sheryl had shut the door behind her. "I can't believe you'd get mixed up with a boy like that. Now everybody at that school will think I'm a terrible mother."

CJ didn't do school for a few days, which was nice. But she wasn't as much fun to play with as she usually was. Sometimes she'd throw a ball for me, I'd bring it back, and she'd completely forget to throw it again. Or she'd stop in the middle of a belly rub to hug me tightly. I didn't mind the hugs, but I wished the belly rubs could last longer.

One of those days she took me over to Trent's house to play with Rocky. "So what's happening?" Trent asked as Rocky and I rolled and wrestled around the yard.

"Well, Shane's expelled. So there's that," CJ said gloomily.

"Good," Trent answered.

"Trent!"

"I mean it, CJ. That guy gives me the creeps."

"Yeah, okay, me, too." CJ sighed. "And I'm not expelled, so that's good, too. But the principal wasn't too happy about the whole thing. He said I showed poor judgment, and I've got to do something to make up for it. So Sheryl said, how about some community service project? And Gloria agreed, as long as nothing about a theft goes on my permanent record. So now I've got to do twenty hours, and I can't go back to art class until I'm done."

Trent shook his head. "Bummer. When you didn't do anything wrong, really."

"No, actually, it's not so bad. Sheryl showed me a list with all these choices. I could either pick up trash along the highway, or pick up trash in the park, or pick up trash at the library, or I can help train dogs. Service dogs!"

I looked up at the word "dog" because often that word goes after "good" or before "treat." Rocky took advantage of the moment to jump on my head.

"So, where are you going to pick up trash?" Trent asked, grinning.

CJ gave him a playful punch on the arm. "You goof."

No praise or treats seemed to be coming. I wiggled out from under Rocky and barked at him so loudly that he took off running, which of course meant I had to chase him.

The next morning CJ got up early. She seemed to be getting ready to do school, which made me sad. But when she went out the front door, she called to me to go with her!

I raced after her. She opened the car door for me, and I leaped into the backseat as quickly as possible, in case she changed her mind. She laughed and got into the front seat, beside Gloria.

I stuck my nose into CJ's ear from behind, and she laughed again.

"You're in a good mood. For a criminal," Gloria said as she started to drive.

CJ was quiet for a minute, looking out the window. Then she said softly, "Molly makes me happy."

Gloria snorted.

They didn't talk much after that.

10

Pretty soon we arrived at a big building, and CJ got out of the car. She let me out, too. I smelled dogs as soon as my paws touched the parking lot. I heard them, too. Inside the building, several big dogs were barking.

A woman came outside to greet us. She was older than CJ but younger than Gloria, and she had long black hair held back by a bright headband. She smelled absolutely wonderful, of dog treats and lots and lots of different dogs.

"Hi, I'm Andi," she said, and then she dropped to her knees and reached for me. "Who's this?"

"This is Molly," CJ said, shifting her weight nervously from foot to foot. "I'm CJ."

"Molly! I had a Molly once. She was a good dog." I wagged enthusiastically. I loved being a good dog. I licked Andi, and she kissed me right back. Most people don't like to kiss a dog's lips, but CJ didn't mind, and Andi didn't, either. "Molly, Molly, Molly," she crooned. "You are so beautiful; yes, you are. What a great dog."

I liked Andi very much.

"What is she, a spaniel-poodle mix?" Andi asked, still petting me.

"Maybe," CJ answered. Her nervousness was melting away. "Her mother was a poodle, but nobody knows about her father. Are you a spoodle, Molly?"

I wagged even harder at my name. Andi stood up, but she kept her hand within reach, and I licked it.

"It's a godsend you're here. I really need the help," Andi said. "Come on inside." We all walked into the building. There was a hallway with kennels on either side, and lots of dogs were in the kennels. They all barked at me and at each other, but I ignored them. Obviously, I was more special than they were, because I got to be outside of the kennels and next to my girl.

"I don't really know anything about training dogs, but I can learn whatever you need," CJ said.

Andi laughed. "Well, okay, but what you're really going to do is free me up so that I can do the training. The dogs need to be watered and fed, and their kennels need

to be cleaned. And they need to be walked outside. Can you handle all that?"

CJ nodded. "But what are you training them to do?" she asked. "I mean, I know they're going to be service dogs. Like, guide dogs or something?"

"Not quite like that," Andi said. "I'm researching cancer detection. Dogs have a sense of smell that's as much as a hundred thousand times better than ours. Some studies have shown that they can detect cancer on a person's breath before any doctor can diagnose it. This could be really important. Early detection is the best way to get to a cure."

"You're training dogs to smell cancer?" There was surprise in CJ's voice.

"Exactly. I'm not the only one doing this, of course, but most of the other experiments have been done in the lab. They let the dog sniff a test tube. I'm thinking, what if it could work on regular people? Like at a health fair, or a community center. So that's what I'm working on. And you . . ."

CJ looked at the kennels of barking dogs. "I'm cleaning up dog poop?"

"You got it," Andi said with a grin.

It was a strange morning.

First CJ took me into a big room and put me in a pen there. Then she brought me another dog to play with, a female with short legs and very long, floppy ears. She was not quite as much fun as Rocky to wrestle and chase with, but she didn't mind when I gave one of her ears a nibble, just to see what it would taste like.

CJ went off and left us both in this pen for a bit. Then she came back, clipped a leash on my collar and one on the other dog's, and took us for a walk. My new friend sat and watched patiently as I chased a squirrel up a tree, put my paws as high on the bark as I could reach, and barked until it jumped to another tree.

Squirrels always do that. So unfair.

I liked playing with a new dog, and I liked going for a walk with CJ. But then she took me back to the pen, took my friend away, and brought me another dog to play with. And we did the same thing again, and again, and again.

CJ's shoes and pants were wetter and wetter each time she came back. She smelled fascinating. The urine of several different dogs was soaked into her clothes. I couldn't stop sniffing her. It was so much fun!

After we'd played like this for a while, CJ clipped the leash on my collar and took me out of the pen. Andi had come into the room while CJ was getting me ready to leave, and she was playing with a big, brown male dog. I dashed over to greet her. CJ stood rubbing her back with both hands and sighing.

I edged up to the brown dog and sniffed under his tail. He sniffed under mine.

"This is Luke," Andi said. "Luke, you like Molly?"

Luke was a serious dog. I could tell. He was focused on the game he was playing with Andi and didn't seem interested in me at all.

There were several metal buckets on the ground. CJ and I watched while Andi took Luke up to one bucket after another. "Smell that?" she said after Luke sniffed one particular bucket. "Now drop!"

Luke lay down. Andi gave him a treat.

I perked my ears up and whined just a little in case Andi had another treat in her pocket.

"That's two hours, right, CJ?" Andi asked.

"Right," CJ said. "Two very exciting hours."

Andi laughed. "I'll sign the form at the end of the week, okay? Thanks. You did a good job."

After that day we often went to Andi's to play with the other dogs, even more often than we went to Trent's house. I liked it. When I walked with CJ and the other dogs, I'd show them what to do if we met a squirrel or a rabbit. When CJ put me in the pen, she'd bring me a friend to play with. Some of the other dogs were great at playing, nearly as good as Rocky. Others were serious, like Luke, and not much interested in chasing or wrestling.

One day, CJ brought me a new friend who just didn't know how to play.

I tried to show him. I snatched up a rubber ball in

my mouth and bowed down with my front legs low and my back legs high. Then I danced away so that he could see I wanted him to chase me.

He didn't seem to understand. He just put his head down low and growled.

I could tell he was sad and frightened, and I knew he'd feel better if we ran around together, playing It's My Ball and You Can't Have It. So I bowed again, and he barked and lunged toward me with his teeth showing.

I was so surprised, I dropped the ball! He grabbed it, which was completely unfair. CJ came right back and snapped a leash on that other dog's collar, and took him to a different pen.

So I didn't have much to do while she was gone except watch Andi play with Luke.

It was a different game from the one with the buckets. Some people sat in metal chairs in different spots in the room. Andi led Luke up to them, one at a time, and he sniffed them.

This didn't look like a very exciting game to me. The people didn't play back! They just sat still. Sometimes humans are like that. They sit and don't do much even when there's a dog right there to play with.

Andi took Luke up to a man with no hair. The big brown dog lay down and crossed his paws. Then he put his head down on them.

"Good dog, Luke!" Andi said. I could hear excitement

in her voice. And she gave Luke a treat, right there on the spot.

Then Andi took Luke away, and the people all got up and changed their seats. It took them a while. When they were done, Andi led Luke back in.

He sniffed all the people again. When he got to the man with no hair, he lay back down. And Andi was thrilled.

"Good dog!" she praised, and she handed out another treat.

I wanted a treat, too. A little saliva dripped out of my mouth as I watched. It didn't seem like a very difficult game to me. I lay down and crossed my front paws and put my head down on them.

Andi didn't even notice.

"Molly, cute girl, are you tired out?" CJ said as she passed my pen. She had the dog who didn't know how to play on a leash.

That's how life is. Some dogs get treats for doing almost nothing, and some dogs are good dogs and get no treats at all.

CJ took the unfriendly dog away, and in a little while she came back and brought me outside for a quick walk of my own. I loved being alone with CJ. The other dogs were fun to play with, but she was my girl, and the times we were together, just the two of us, were best.

When we went back inside, the people were still sitting in chairs, and Andi was playing with a new yellow dog. I trotted over to the bald man's chair.

He bent down to smile at me. "Cute dog," he said softly. His voice sounded like he didn't have a lot of strength.

His breath came out with a funny smell to it. For some reason, I didn't like it much. Most smells are amazing. Other dogs' urine, the trash in the trash can, something dead by the roadside—they are all so interesting that I always long to get my mouth on whatever smells so incredible.

This smell, though, I didn't care for. It made me think of a time I'd dug something shiny and crunchy out of the trash can at home. It had smelled salty and delicious, but when I'd tried chewing it, the taste in my mouth was horrible. And it had lingered even after I'd gulped down half a bowl of water.

This man's breath smelled like that. Still, if Luke got a treat, I wanted a treat. I lay down and crossed my paws, putting my head on them.

"Look at that!" Andi said. She came up to me. "Hey, Molly, did you learn to do that from Luke?"

I wagged happily, sure that a treat was coming. But it didn't.

I really liked Andi. She smelled wonderful, and she

always hugged me when CJ brought me here to play. But I did think it was very unfair of her to give Luke a treat and not me, when we'd done the exact same thing.

The next time we came back, though, I decided that Andi was not so bad after all. She talked to CJ for a little while and then decided to play with me.

To be honest, it was not my favorite game. After all, there are ropes to tug on and balls to chase. Why just sniff people in chairs? But humans are like that. Their idea of play is usually not as much fun as a dog's. You have to put up with it, though, if you want treats.

Andi had CJ hold my leash, and we walked up to a woman sitting in a chair, a woman who had on fur boots that smelled like cats. "Hi, what's your name?" she said, holding down her hand for me to lick.

"This is Molly," Andi said. I wagged,

And that was all there was to this game. We went up to all the people in their chairs. Each one petted me and talked to me a little, but none gave me any treats, even though I could smell that one man had something with cheese on it in one of his pockets.

Then we came to a woman whose hands smelled like fish. She leaned over to pet me, and I picked up the same scent I'd noticed on the bald man.

"Hello, Molly," the woman said.

I licked at her hands, and then we started to move

on to the next person. I felt the slightest hint of tension in Andi, and that's when I got it.

I wasn't just supposed to lie down when I was next to the bald man. It was that smell. This game had something to do with that smell. I turned back to the woman and lay down, crossing my paws.

"That's it!" said Andi, clapping her hands. "Good dog, Molly. Good dog!"

A treat at last!

11

I was a good dog when we played with Andi and I lay down at the right time. But I was a bad dog later on at home. And I didn't even know what I had done!

"Bath, Molly!" CJ called.

I didn't know what she meant, but I heard my name, so I wagged and ran to her. She took me by the collar and tugged me into the bathroom. Then she pushed me into a sort of long, low box with smooth sides.

I knew this box. Lots of times CJ and Gloria stood inside it and let water run all over them. I don't know why they liked to do this, but human beings are very strange sometimes.

It didn't smell very interesting, though. I squirmed under CJ's hands so I could get out and we could go outside and play. Maybe go to the park or visit Trent and Rocky.

"No, Molly, hold still!" CJ said. I knew she wanted me to do something, so I licked her face.

She laughed. "Oh, Molly. Hold still now." She had a sort of metal dog bowl in there with a long handle sticking out of it. I lapped at it, but the water was warm and not very tasty. Besides, I wasn't thirsty.

CJ scooped some of the water up and poured it on my head.

I yipped in surprise and shook my head hard. My ears flapped.

"No, Molly. You have to hold still!" CJ said more sternly.

I still wasn't sure what she wanted. But her hands were heavy on me, and I lowered my head and didn't move, feeling like a bad dog as she poured water all over me from the dog dish.

Then—even worse—she rubbed some foul-smelling soap into my fur.

"You're going to look so beautiful for the art show," she crooned as she worked. "That's a good girl, Molly, just a little longer. You're a good dog."

Surely not! Good dogs got treats and petting and hugs. They did not get treated like this! All of the delicious scents my fur had gathered over time—dirt and old food and dust from the carpet—escaped down the drain with the warm water. I whined and tried to slip out of CJ's hands, but my claws just scrabbled uselessly on the smooth surface of the box. CJ got a better grip on me.

"I just have to rinse you, Molly!" she said, and she poured more water over me from my nose to my drooping tail.

But then, it seemed, I wasn't a bad dog anymore, because CJ let me go and grabbed a big towel. She wrapped it all around me and pulled me close to her. "Oh, Molly dog, oh, Molly dog, you are a schnoodle schnoodle dog," she whispered, and I knew I was a good dog now, and that my girl loved me.

She rubbed me up and down with the towel until my skin felt so alive and buzzing that, when she let me go, I just had to run. I raced around the house, shaking myself to get rid of any last drops of that stinky, soapy water and leaping over chairs and on the couch. Then I flopped onto the carpet and scooted along, rubbing my belly and then my shoulders and then my back, until I began to smell like myself again and all the dampness was gone from my fur.

"What is that dog *doing*?" Gloria asked, standing in the doorway between the kitchen and the living room.

"She's just happy!" CJ said. She was smiling and holding my brush. "Come here, Molly. Come and get brushed!"

"Outside!" Gloria said.

So CJ took me outside and brushed me until I was

wiggling with pleasure. Then we went back in, and it was CJ's turn inside the box with the water.

I lay on a towel, waiting for her, and wondering if CJ was a bad girl like I'd been a bad dog. But she didn't seem sad about the water. When she got out, she brushed her hair like she'd brushed mine, and then she pointed something at her head that made a horrible, whining sound. I'd heard it before—it sounded like something being hurt—so I ran away and hid under the blankets on her bed until she was finished.

CJ found me there and pulled me out, and tied some sort of string around my neck. "There, Molly," she said.

I nibbled at one end of the string. It did not taste very interesting, but it was better than nothing.

"No, Molly." CJ pulled the string out of my mouth. "Don't eat your ribbon!"

"CJ! Come and let me see what you have on!" Gloria called from her bedroom.

CJ went. I lay on the bed and got to work with my teeth, seeing if I could get the string completely off my neck.

I could hear bits and pieces of the conversation between Gloria and CJ as I chewed. "What's wrong with the dress I picked?" CJ said.

"Well, obviously. Obviously," Gloria said. "No, try on the blue one. Let me see."

"But I like the red one."

"Red is not your color, Clarity."

"But it's *my* painting that's in the art show, right?"

"And you're *my* daughter, and you're not going in that horrible baggy red thing. It makes you look like you've gained ten pounds."

I had the ribbon almost off now, but it somehow got stuck on one of my teeth. I had to twist my neck to yank it loose. When I got that over with, I could hear CJ's voice again. I wagged, just because it was so nice to hear my girl. Even if she didn't sound very happy.

"Makeup? Gloria, do I have to?"

"Hold still. Close your eyes. You have my eyes, you know, if you'd just do something with them."

"I do. I see things with them."

"Just. Be. Quiet. Clarity," Gloria said, kind of growling.

Then the doorbell rang. I jumped off the bed with the string still trailing from my neck and ran to do my job and bark. CJ hurried to the hallway, too. She grabbed my collar and opened the door.

"Yes?" she panted.

"Your mom here?" asked the man standing on the porch.

"Well—" CJ hesitated.

"Gus!" Gloria said from behind us. She was wearing clattery shoes that made a lot of noise on the floor of the hallway. "Gus, come in. How nice to see you. Clarity, this is Gus. My boyfriend."

The man stepped inside. Since he was in the house, it wasn't my job to bark at him anymore, so I sniffed his shoes. They smelled like grass and sweat, and something sweet had been spilled on the left one. I licked it up.

"What's on that dog's neck?" the man asked.

"Um. A ribbon," CJ mumbled. "Boyfriend?"

"Used to be a ribbon, maybe," the man said.

"Of course!" Gloria said.

"You never said anything . . ." CJ looked at Gloria. I licked her fingers, and she tugged the ribbon off my neck. Thank goodness that game was over.

"Well, I don't tell you everything!" Gloria said brightly, and laughed. The man called Gus laughed, too. Then CJ and Gloria went back to their rooms while Gus sat on the couch and tapped one foot impatiently. Finally, CJ and Gloria came back out, and all the people gathered by the door. CJ was wearing a pair of those loud shoes, too.

It looked like they were getting ready to go out, and I ran over in case they wanted me to go with them. Often that didn't happen, but I was always prepared.

"That's right, Molly. It's your night, too!" CJ said, and she picked my leash from a hook on the wall.

I danced around happily. "Clarity, really!" Gloria grumbled, and CJ clipped the leash on, and finally we all went outside. I never understood why it takes people so long to get outside, but never mind that. I was going somewhere with my girl!

Gloria and Gus got in a car. CJ opened the back door and called me in. She got in, too, and fastened a strap around herself. I flopped across her lap, panting happily.

"Don't let that dog get hair all over that dress!" Gloria called back.

"I won't," CJ said quietly.

"So how long does this art show thing go on for?" Gus asked as he started driving.

"Oh, not very long. An hour. Of course, Clarity might have to talk to some people at the museum. Press, you know."

"Mom!" CJ said, horrified. "It's just a show of work by kids. It's not some big thing!"

"Clarity June, really. It is a big thing. You were the only student from your school to get a painting in, weren't you?" Gloria said.

"Well, yes, but—"

"I knew you'd be talented. Even when you were a baby," Gloria said. She sounded very happy. "It runs in families, you know. I had quite a successful singing career before Clarity was born, Gus."

"Yeah?"

"Oh, certainly. Of course, everything is different when you've had a child. But I wasn't surprised to get that letter from your art teacher. Not surprised at all."

CJ lowered her head to hug me. Gloria chattered away and Gus answered her, but CJ didn't say anything. Maybe she wished she could ride in the front seat, too. I could understand that. I liked it better when I got to be a front-seat dog as well.

"Pull in there," Gloria said to Gus, pointing.

Gus stopped the car. I jumped up to look out the window and wagged hard, banging CJ in the face with my tail. We were at Trent's house!

A moment later, one of the car doors opened, and Trent slid in beside CJ and me. It seemed like there wasn't going to be any playing or wrestling with Rocky, though, because Gus began driving again right away. Too bad.

"Hey, Molly. Hi, CJ," Trent said. "Wow, you look . . ."

"Gloria did my makeup," CJ mumbled.

"Wow," Trent said again. Then he got quiet, too, and looked out of the window. I lay down so my front legs were on CJ and my back legs were on Trent. They both petted me. Sometimes their hands bumped.

Then Gus stopped the car again, and we all got out and went inside a really big building, even bigger than the place where we played with Andi or the one where we went to do art. And there were lots of people standing around. Some of them were talking. Others were staring at the walls.

People really do very strange things.

CJ kept hold of my leash, so I stayed close beside her. She and Trent went over to one particular wall and looked at it.

"It's a great painting, CJ," Trent said.

CJ shifted her weight from foot to foot. "Stop. You're embarrassing me."

"Come on. You must know how good it is. Here, let me take a picture of you, okay? You stand there with Molly, right next to the painting. The artist and her model!"

Trent backed away and held out a little rectangular box. CJ rolled her eyes. Then she picked me up and held me close to her face, smiling.

"That's great," said Trent. "Molly has just the same expression on her face as she does in your painting. You can really see how you got just what she looks like."

Trent's box made a little noise, and then CJ set me down. My girl and Trent wandered around for a bit, looking at some more walls, while I sniffed at feet and legs and noticed that a lot of the people had drinks or napkins in their hands. Sometimes they dropped little bits of cheese or chunks of crackers. I was happy to clean those up.

Against one wall of the room was a table with more food. I wished CJ would head over there. I looked up at her to see if she had any intention of going where the food was, and then I felt her stiffen.

"There's Sheryl," she whispered to Trent.

CJ sounded nervous. I took a look around to see if there was a threat that I should know about.

"So? I thought you liked her," Trent said quietly.

"I did. I do. But what if she's mad at me? About the thing with Shane?"

"CJ, you're nuts. She stood up for you with the principal, didn't she? She entered your painting in this show. So why do you think she's mad?"

"I don't know," CJ said. "I just . . ."

"She's coming over. Chill out. It'll be fine."

"Hello, CJ," said a familiar voice. It was Sheryl, from when we did art building! "Hello, Molly."

I wagged furiously. "Oh. Um," mumbled CJ, twisting my leash in her hand. "Hi, Sheryl."

"We've missed you in art class," Sheryl said. "Will you be coming back when the community service is over?"

"I don't know," CJ said awkwardly.

I pressed close to my girl's knees, trying to comfort her.

"I hope so," Sheryl said. Her voice was warm. "Class isn't as good without you. And of course everybody wants to see Molly again!"

Sheryl bent down to pet me. I felt CJ relax a little, and I wagged again as Sheryl rubbed both hands along my ears.

"Such a famous girl tonight!" she said.

I could smell cheese on her breath, and crackers, and something else, something familiar. I knew what to do.

I lay down with my paws crossed, and lowered my head onto them.

"Oh, how cute," Sheryl said, smiling.

CJ drew in her breath with a gasp of horror.

No one remembered to give me a treat.

12

CJ whispered, "Excuse me," to Sheryl. She grabbed Trent by the arm and pulled him away. Since she still had my leash in her hand, I went with her as well.

That was lucky, because someone had spilled a sweet-tasting drink, and I was able to lap it up while CJ talked to Trent in quick, low words.

"You're kidding," Trent said.

"I'm not kidding!"

"You think she has cancer? And Molly can tell? Seriously?"

"I mean it, Trent. In Andi's experiments, Molly gets it right every time."

"That's crazy. Sorry. I don't mean *you're* crazy. I just

133

mean—" Trent shook his head. "It's just so wild, you know? That Molly can tell something like that?"

"But, Trent, what do I do?" CJ asked.

I looked up. My girl was worried. I could hear it in her voice. Even her smell had changed. I gave one last lick to the sticky floor and went to nuzzle at her hand, to remind her that everything was all right, since I was there.

CJ stroked my head, but she clearly wasn't paying real attention to me. I had to keep nudging her hand because she'd pet me once and then let her hand just hang there, doing nothing in particular.

"Should I tell her?" CJ said.

"Well, you have to tell her," Trent said.

"But here? Now? It's an art show. There are all these people."

"She's got to know, CJ. And it's not like there's ever going to be a good time."

I felt a little of CJ's worry ease. She stood a bit straighter.

"You're right. Okay." She nodded. "Oh no. Look over there."

"What?"

"Sheryl's talking to Gloria. I can't believe it. Of all people . . ."

"I'll come with you, if you want," Trent offered.

"No, wait for me here, okay? Sheryl probably won't

want an audience. I'll figure out a way to get her away from Gloria. Come on, Molly."

I stuck close to CJ's side as we made our way through all the people. Even when someone dropped a cracker right in front of me, I didn't swerve to eat it. I could tell my girl needed me.

Sheryl was standing and talking to Gloria when CJ reached her side. Gus was at Gloria's side with a glass in his hand. "Sheryl?" CJ said nervously. "Can I talk to you? Right now?"

Sheryl looked a little surprised, but she smiled in a kind way. "Of course, if it's important," she said.

"It's kind of private," CJ told her.

"Private!" Gloria stood up straighter. "I'm your own mother, Clarity June. What's private from me?"

CJ squirmed a little. Sheryl looked back and forth from her to Gloria. Gus frowned.

"We won't be a minute," Sheryl told Gloria, and she reached out to take CJ's arm. They walked across the room, toward the doors. Maybe we were going outside! A walk would be more fun than staying in the room, even with the occasional bit of food on the floor.

When they got to the doorway, CJ talked. Sheryl listened. She shook her head. Sheryl grew paler and put out a hand to touch the door frame, as if she needed to lean on it for support.

"I don't know, I can't be sure, maybe Molly's wrong," CJ said in a rush. "Except she's never been wrong in the experiments. I just . . . I had to tell you. You should go to the doctor right away. Andi, she's the dog trainer, she says early detection is a really big deal, the biggest deal there is."

Sheryl's eyes were wide and bright. "My mother—she died of breast cancer," she murmured. A few tears started to slip down her cheeks.

"I'm sorry. I'm really sorry, Sheryl," CJ said. She sounded like she might cry, too.

I looked back and forth from one to the other. Both of them were worried and anxious. And we didn't seem to be going on a walk. I wondered why not. I was sure a walk would make us all feel better.

"I have to . . . I have to go," Sheryl said. More tears came down her face. "I'm sorry, CJ, I just can't—I have to leave. Now."

And she pushed her way out of the door, moving like she couldn't see very well.

I put a paw on CJ's leg to get her attention. Then a voice spoke from behind us.

"What on earth was that all about, Clarity?"

It was Gloria. Gus was right behind her.

Gloria stood looking at us with her lips pinched together. "What did you say to that teacher?" she said, her voice low. "Whatever it was, you certainly caused a scene."

CJ rubbed a hand over her face. "I had to tell her something, Gloria. It was important."

Trent began pushing his way toward us from across the room where CJ had left him.

"Isn't that just like you, Clarity," Gloria said impatiently. "Because something's important to you, you think it must be important to everyone else. But it's time you started to grow up and think a little about other people. It's embarrassing to me to have you behave like this."

"CJ *was* thinking about other people," Trent said angrily, coming up behind Gloria and Gus. "You don't know what happened. She did the right thing."

"Trent, stop," CJ said wearily. "You'll just make it worse."

Everybody was upset. Nobody was eating any food. Nobody was petting me. Nobody was even looking at the walls anymore. Instead, lots of people in the room were staring at us.

I would never understand why people spent so much time standing around and making words at each other when those words didn't seem to make them happy.

Gus looked at Trent. "Kid, go look at the art some more."

Trent's jaw set in a stubborn way. He looked like Rocky when my brother was getting ready to plow into me and knock me over.

"Just go," CJ said softly to Trent. "It's okay. Please."

Trent let out a long breath and walked away. Not very far away, though. He stood looking at a wall with his hands in his pockets.

"Now, let me handle this," Gus said to Gloria.

"Gladly. I'm going to get myself something to drink," Gloria answered. She turned around on the heel of her loud shoes. She walked over to the tables where there was food.

I looked at CJ to see if we'd be doing the same thing.

Instead, Gus took CJ by the arm and pulled her out the door.

CJ was so startled that she dropped my leash. But that didn't matter, because of course I went with her. Gus shut the door so quickly it nearly caught my tail.

"Let go!" CJ protested.

I felt the fur on the back of my neck start to rise.

"Listen," Gus said to CJ. "I don't know what's going on, but I do know one thing. You're going to start talking to your mother with respect. Hear me?"

CJ was twisting and pulling at her arm, trying to get it out of Gus's grip. "You're right. You *don't* know what's going on!" she said angrily. "So leave me alone!"

I'd never bitten anyone before. I'd never even really had to threaten anyone. Sure, Rocky and I would growl when we played, and I made sure to bark when someone rang the doorbell, but those were not real threats. More just letting everyone know that I *could* be fierce if I needed to.

Now I needed to.

Somehow I knew just what to do. I put my head down low and felt my lips pulling back to show my teeth. Slowly, I walked toward Gus.

"Hey!" Gus dropped CJ's arm just as the door opened behind us.

"Clarity June, I hope you're ready to behave in a civilized manner now," Gloria said. Then she gasped. "*What* is going on here?"

Gus backed away from me. CJ dropped to her knees and caught hold of me.

"It's okay, Molly. It's okay, Molly," she whispered.

There were tears on her face. I licked them off. They were salty and also had a funny taste from a black streak that ran along her cheeks. But she was calmer now, and I felt the fur along my back settled down where it belonged.

"That dog's vicious," Gus said angrily. He went down the steps, heading toward the sidewalk. "That's it. I'm out of here."

"Gus!" Gloria called after him. "Come back!"

I knew that word. I looked up at Gloria, but I could tell that she did not want me to come to her. She was looking at me with horror.

"Gloria, listen." CJ lifted up her face from my fur. "Molly was—"

"I don't want to hear about it!" Gloria said. "We're leaving now, Clarity. I'll go get the car."

"But, Mom—"

"Not another word!"

"But Trent! We have to get Trent! He needs a ride home!"

"Oh." Gloria hesitated.

"I'll go get him." CJ got to her feet.

"You certainly will not! You look dreadful. We can't let anyone see you like that. *I'll* go. You get in the car. We'll talk at home."

Gus didn't ride home with us. Everybody in the car was very quiet. A few times Trent opened his mouth, but CJ shook her head at him, and he closed it again.

Trent got out of the car at his house. CJ, Gloria, and I went home.

"That dog," Gloria said as soon as we got into the living room, "is dangerous."

"Molly is *not* dangerous!" CJ nearly shouted.

"I saw it with my own eyes, Clarity! She was going to bite Gus!"

"Only to protect me!"

"Protect you!" Gloria snorted. "Why would *you* need protection?"

"He grabbed my arm, Gloria! He wouldn't let go!"

"That is ridiculous. Gus is a gentleman. Anyway, we are not talking about Gus. We are talking about *that dog*."

She pointed at me. Her voice was tight and angry, but I could sense fear in its high pitch and in her widened eyes.

I started to go closer to her, looking around to see if I could discover what was making her so afraid. I wanted Gloria to know that I'd protect her, too. She wasn't as close to me as CJ—she wasn't my girl—but she lived here in the house with us. I wouldn't let anyone hurt her.

"Get her away from me!" Gloria shrieked.

CJ caught hold of my collar. "She isn't going to do anything to you, Gloria!"

"I want her out. Outside! Put her in the yard, Clarity June. This instant! Then we are going to talk more!"

"Okay, okay," CJ said. She pulled at my collar, and I followed her out into the yard. Maybe we would stay there and chase balls or roll in the grass. Anything would be better than more of those angry, frightened words.

CJ bent low and put both her hands on my head. She kissed me.

"Don't worry, Molly," my girl whispered. "I won't let her do anything to you."

Then she slipped back through the door into the house and shut it in my face.

I was so astonished, I sat down in the grass and didn't even bark.

What had happened? Why had my girl left me out here in the yard?

This didn't make sense. I could tell that CJ needed me. She was upset and worried and afraid. Maybe nobody was pulling on her arm right now, but there was still something making her feel anxious. And I needed to help.

I remembered what to do. I barked to let CJ know she'd made a mistake and left me outside. Then I waited for the door to open.

It didn't open.

This was very strange. I barked some more, as loudly as I could. Then I scratched at the door, trying to see if I could push it open myself. It didn't move.

So I kept barking.

Surely CJ would figure it out. She'd come to get me. This wasn't like the old days, when she'd leave me under the stairs. That time was over. She'd be back to get me. She'd be back *soon*.

But it wasn't soon. It was a very long time before CJ came back.

Everything was dark and all the lights in the neighborhood houses were out when a last—*at last!*—the door creaked open.

"Molly!" CJ whispered.

I raced to the door and threw myself inside, leaping on my girl. She sat on the kitchen floor, holding me on

her lap while I licked her face frantically, trying to let her know how long it had taken her to come and get me.

"Shhh, Molly, shhh," CJ whispered. "Quiet, Molly, quiet. You have to be quiet."

I knew that old command. I sat down in CJ's lap and looked up at her face in appeal. Surely we weren't going to play that game anymore, were we? I thought CJ had learned her lesson about that!

It seemed I was right. What a relief! CJ took me up in her arms and carried me up the stairs to her bedroom. She moved slowly and cautiously from each step to the next, and tiptoed down the hall to her bedroom.

Once we were there, she tucked me under the covers. Because I felt that my girl still needed me to watch over her, I lay curled against her side. She rested a hand on my fur. I stayed awake until her body relaxed against mine, and I heard her breathing grow soft and deep.

Then I fell asleep, too, where I belonged, next to my girl.

13

The next morning, while the house was still quiet and dark, CJ picked me up and hurried down the stairs with me. She took me into the backyard again, and brought my food and water bowls out there, too. Then she went inside.

I tried a bark or two, reminding her to come and get me. But then I got busy eating my breakfast, and after breakfast I was full enough to curl up in the grass for a little nap. I woke when CJ hurried outside once more, wearing her backpack. She knelt and hugged me and kissed me. "Don't worry, Molly," she whispered. "I'll think of something." And then she ran out of the gate and down the sidewalk.

I'd figured out that, when CJ wore her backpack, she

was going to do school and would not be home for a while. I returned to my nap.

A while later, the door creaked open.

It seemed early for CJ to be back. I looked up in surprise. No CJ. Gloria stood in the doorway.

I could tell she was still afraid. I got to my feet, sniffing, and checked all around the yard for a threat, but I couldn't find a thing.

"Want a piece of roast beef?" Gloria said.

I took a step toward her, then stopped. I could hear the question in her voice, but I didn't know if it meant I was in trouble or not.

"Here," she said. She tossed something in the grass a few feet in front of me. My nose twitched as a delicious smell reached it—rich and savory and wonderful. I bounded over to the piece of meat that Gloria had dropped and snatched it up, eating it in two bites.

Marvelous!

I looked back up at Gloria. I tried wagging my tail, to see how she'd respond.

"Want another one?" she asked. She pitched a second piece to me.

I jumped to it and ate it, too. I must be a good dog, to get two treats at once!

Then Gloria shut the door. I sat down and sighed. No more treats?

About a minute later, Gloria called from the front of the house. "Yoo-hoo, Molly! Dog, want another treat?"

I knew my name! I knew the word "dog"! I knew "treat"! I bounded over to the gate and found that it was open. Happily, I trotted along the side of the house to the front yard. Gloria was standing in the driveway.

"Treat," she said again. I wagged harder. She tossed a piece of meat in my direction. This time I was ready for it, and I leaped to snag it out of the air. This was a wonderful game! As far as I was concerned, we could play it forever.

Gloria opened the door to the backseat of the car. "Okay, want to get in, dog? Treat?"

I thought I understood what she meant. Something to do with treats and the car. Hesitantly, I made my way over to the open door. Gloria tossed two pieces of meat on the floor of the backseat, and I scrambled in. I heard the car door slam behind me as I ate.

Then Gloria got into the front seat and started the car. We drove off.

I finished my treats and hopped up onto the seat. Gloria gave a nervous little gasp and looked around at me, but then returned her attention to the road. I stared out the window for a while, wishing it was open so that I could stick my nose in the crack and drink in all the rushing smells that were passing by. But the window was closed, and it was no fun smelling the glass. Plus, my belly was full, and it seemed there would be no more treats right now. I curled up on the seat for my second nap of the morning.

After I'd had a nice sleep, I felt the car stop. I stood up and shook myself, my collar rattling. The sound of the engine died away. The car became still.

Gloria twisted around in her seat so that I could see her face. "Careful now," she said. "Remember, I fed you a treat? You be nice, Molly."

I wagged at my name and the word "treat." Gloria's hands reached for me over the seat. I sniffed at them. They still smelled good, but there was no meat in them. I heard a sudden click, and my collar dropped off and landed on the seat between my front paws.

I lowered my nose and gave it a good sniff. It was hard to smell the thing when it was hanging around my neck. But it mostly smelled like me, and that was not too interesting. I already knew what I smelled like.

Gloria got out of the car and opened my door. "Come along. Heel. Be a good dog. Don't run off," she said.

I wagged for being a good dog and jumped out of the car.

We were in a parking lot. There was a strong odor of dogs everywhere. I looked all around, but I couldn't see any of the dogs who'd clearly been here not long before.

Gloria began walking toward a building. I followed

her. The scent of dogs became stronger and stronger. And they did not smell happy. I could smell fear and loneliness and anger, and it made me nervous. I crowded closer to Gloria's heels. She started walking quicker.

Together, we hurried through a door. Gloria let it shut behind us. We were in a small room with a desk; behind the desk was a second door, this one open. Through it I could hear more than a dozen dogs barking. And the smell was even worse here. I backed toward the door to the parking lot, hoping we'd go home soon. CJ was probably waiting for me.

"Hello? Hello?" Gloria called.

A woman came through the open door. She smiled. "Yes? Can I help you?"

"I found this poor dog abandoned in the streets," Gloria said. "There's no telling how long he's been living like that, alone and far, far away from his family. Is this where you drop off lost dogs?"

Gloria and the woman talked for a few minutes, and then Gloria left. The door swished shut behind her.

I looked after her, a little puzzled. Gloria wasn't like CJ—she wasn't my girl—but I had a feeling I should have gone with her. I went over to the door and barked once. Maybe she'd forgotten about me? Would she come back and open the door?

The new woman came up to me and offered me her hand to sniff. She smelled like soap and other dogs. I gave her a quick sniff and a lick, just to be polite, but I wasn't very interested. I wanted Gloria to come back so we could leave.

The new woman put a new collar around my neck. "Come on, now, girl," she said.

She walked away. I stayed by the door.

"Come on," she said again, and she reached out and tugged at my new collar. I got the idea that I was supposed to go with her. It was confusing, but I wanted to be a good dog. I followed her through the other door.

The place where the new woman took me was a little like the room where CJ and I sometimes played with Andi. There were pens there, and lots of dogs. But no people sitting in chairs for me to sniff. And no Andi. And no CJ.

The woman put me in a pen with a cement floor. Then she shut the door and left.

I stared after her in astonishment. What was going on here?

Someone, somewhere, had made a mistake. I was sure of it.

Inside the cage, there was a wooden box with a roof and a door. I poked my head inside, just to see what it was like. A piece of carpet was on the floor of the box, and obviously several other dogs had slept there before I got here.

None of them had been happy.

I pulled my head out of the box and looked around. The place was filled with the sound of barking. Tiny dogs yipped. Big dogs bayed and bellowed. To my right was an empty cage; to my left was a large brown hound with floppy ears who lay on the cement floor, occasionally putting up his head and opening his mouth to join in the din.

I barked a little, too. I couldn't help it. But no one came to let me out of the cage.

No one came to let *any* of the dogs out. But we could not help barking anyway, letting the humans know what they should do.

At last all the barking seemed to have an effect. The woman who'd put me in this cage came back. I rushed to her, wagging frantically, and to my delight she opened the door of my cage.

Thank goodness she'd come to let me out. I didn't like being here. It was loud, and the cement floor was cold, and I wanted to be close to CJ. If I couldn't play with her and feel her hands in my fur, at least I wanted to curl up in her bed and sniff the sheets that smelled like her and wait like a good dog for her to be done doing school and come back home.

But the woman didn't seem to understand that I needed to go home to my girl. Deftly, she blocked the door with her body, trapping me inside. Then she set a bowl of food and another of water on the floor of my cage.

Reaching in, she petted me gently, but she wouldn't let me get out. Then she shut the cage door again.

I sniffed at the food, but I wasn't hungry. I'd emptied my dog bowl in the backyard and had all those pieces of meat besides. Anyway, I missed CJ so much that I couldn't even care about food.

I found myself pacing back and forth, whimpering a little. Then I crawled into the box with the carpet inside and tried to sleep, but it was impossible.

The barking that filled the air was full of fear. It had some anger in it, too, some sadness, some pain. When I barked, I could hear my own plea to be let out of the cage, to run, to play, to find my girl again.

Hours went past. CJ still didn't come to get me. The woman brought me fresh water once. Then the lights were turned off. Some of the dogs slept, but I didn't, not much. I couldn't. I pictured myself lying at the foot of CJ's bed. I longed for the touch of her hands on my fur and the familiar and wonderful scent of her skin.

In the morning, a man came with fresh food. I ate a few bites while he watched from outside the cage. Then he opened the door again.

I looked up alertly, tensing my muscles, ready to spring out. But he blocked the door just as the woman had done yesterday. He reached out and snapped a leash onto my collar.

And then—my heart leaped with joy!—he held the door to my cage open.

I threw myself outside and tried to run, but the leash snapped me back. I didn't care about the pressure around my neck. I leaned into the leash as hard as I could until I was nearly towing the man down the hall. All the other dogs barked and barked as we went past.

The man brought me to a small room where a woman was waiting. She boosted me up on a slick metal table, just as CJ would do when I went to Dr. Marty's. I didn't mind the vet so much if CJ was there with me, but this was all strange and new. I held my ears and my tail low to show I was no threat, hoping that no one would hurt me. And maybe the woman understood, because she patted me and spoke in a low, gentle voice.

Then the man took hold of my head, holding me on both sides of my face so that I couldn't move. The woman picked up a stick and moved it close to my head. Was it a toy to chew? I didn't know. The man held on, and I couldn't get a good look.

"Got a hit," the woman said.

"I knew she'd be chipped," the man said.

Then he boosted me down and took me back to my cage.

My cage! I couldn't believe it. I thought these people had understood that this cage was no place for me.

Instead they'd brought me straight back! I was too disappointed even to walk the few steps to the box and the scrap of carpet. I just flopped to the cold cement floor with a groan. I chewed on the edge of the doghouse a little, but even that did not make me feel better.

A few hours later the man came back. "Hello, Molly," he said from the door to my cage.

He'd said my name. My name! Just hearing it seemed to bring CJ closer to me. She was the one who said my name most often and with the most love. I sat up, wagging.

He opened the door. When I ran to him, he clipped a leash to my collar. "Come on, girl. Someone's here to see you."

The man took me down the hall between rows of frantic, barking dogs. The minute he opened the door at the end I could smell the scent I loved most in the world. CJ was here at last!

I barreled into the small room where I'd last seen Gloria, pulling my leash right out of the man's hand. My girl! My girl had come! She was standing near the door. I threw myself at her, and she fell to her knees and put her arms around me.

"Molly. Molly. Oh, Molly," she said.

I kissed her face and then wiggled free. It was so wonderful to be held by CJ that I could have stayed forever, but at the same time, I was so excited that I simply had to run.

I tore around and around CJ, the leash trailing behind me and winding around my girl. My relief and happiness came out in little whimpering barks. CJ laughed and wiped her face. "Good dog, Molly. You sit. Sit, now."

I touched my rear end briefly to the ground and then leaped back into CJ's lap.

She laughed more. "No, Molly, it's okay. You sit. Molly, sit." Reluctantly, I slithered out of her lap and sat. She stood up and I inched over without getting up so that I was sitting on her feet while she talked to the man.

"I've been so worried," she said. "The gate to the backyard was open somehow. I'm sure I locked it when I left for school, but somehow it was open when I came home."

"Good thing you had her microchipped," the man said. "The woman who dropped her off said she was just running down the street."

"That's not like Molly," CJ said, shaking her head. "I wish I knew what happened. Wait, what woman?"

"The lady who found her and brought her here," the man said. "Some rich lady."

"Rich?" CJ asked.

"Well, you know. She had a new car, expensive clothes. Lots of perfume. Nice hair. You could just tell she had money."

"Blonde hair?" CJ asked slowly.

"Yeah."

CJ took something out of her pocket. I perked up, checking to see if it was a treat, but it was just a flat box that smelled like metal and plastic. Nothing interesting there.

"Was this her?" CJ asked.

The man looked at the little box. "Hey, yeah. That's her. You know her?"

CJ put the little box back in her pocket. "Yes," she said tightly. And she wasn't as happy as she had been before, which was very strange, considering that she and I were together again at last.

She and the man talked a little more, and then she took me out into the parking lot. As soon as we were out the door, CJ crouched down and put her arms around me.

I licked her face eagerly.

"Oh, Molly, Molly," CJ whispered. "You silly schnoodle not a poodle. I was scared something awful had happened to you." She felt sad, so I pressed close to her, letting her know that everything was fine now. "I'm so, so sorry," CJ said. "I didn't know she'd do something like this."

CJ and I walked a little way down the street, and then we stood there for a while, as if we were waiting for something. Finally, a giant car pulled to a halt in front of us with a loud puff and some squealing. A door opened up, and CJ talked to the driver for a while.

"No, she's not a service dog, but she'll be good," CJ said. "She's really good. She can sit on my lap. Please let her on the bus; I have to get her home."

When they were done talking, CJ took me up some stairs to a place with lots of seats. I sat on her lap and looked out a window. CJ pulled it down for me a little bit so I could press my nose to the crack and sniff as much as I wanted.

When we got home, CJ fed me. I was happy to eat even though I'd already gotten a bowlful of food in my cage. Then we sat together on the couch in the living room. It was wonderful to be so close to my girl again, smelling her, feeling her warmth, letting her hands scratch at my neck and rub along my back from my ears to my tail.

But I could tell that CJ was not as happy as I was. She was still worried about something. "Oh, Molly," she whispered every now and then. "What are we going do to?"

I would wag hard and lick whatever part of her I could reach.

After a while, I heard the scratch of a key in the door. Normally, it was one of my jobs to run to the door when it opened, but this time I didn't want to get off CJ's lap.

Gloria walked into the living room and stood still, staring at CJ and me. She dropped her purse on the floor.

"The shelter called," CJ said. She held on to me tightly and looked defiantly up at her mother. "They read Molly's microchip. I went and got her."

Gloria didn't answer.

"I know what you did, Gloria. I know what you did!" CJ shouted. "How could you?"

After that there was a lot more shouting. Eventually, CJ pushed me off her lap to stand up. I leaped off the couch, too, and pressed against her legs. Gloria backed across the room.

"I'm not having that dog in the house. I'm not! She's dangerous!" Gloria insisted.

CJ got quiet. She stood still, looking at her mother. I looked back and forth from CJ to Gloria and yawned with anxiety.

"Do you hear me, Clarity June? This is my house, and I don't want that dog in it!"

"Fine," CJ said quietly.

She was not shouting anymore, but I could still feel the tension that ran through her body.

"Just leave us together for today," CJ said. She sat down beside me and pulled me onto her lap. "Just one more day. Then I promise you'll never see Molly again."

14

The next morning, CJ fed me out in the back-yard once more. Then she hurried inside. When she came back she was wearing her backpack, ready to do school. Again.

This time her backpack was bigger than usual, and I could tell by the way that she walked that it was heavy on her shoulders. And something wonderful happened next.

"Come on, Molly," CJ whispered. "But be quiet."

She snapped my leash on my collar and led me out of the gate, into the front yard, and down the sidewalk.

I was going to do school with my girl!

I was so happy that I jumped and leaped at the end of the leash. CJ kept saying, "Shhh," which I supposed meant that she was as happy as I was. We were together! And the grass smelled fascinating! And there was a squirrel to bark at on a branch overhead!

"Quiet, Molly!" CJ insisted, and she pulled me around the corner. Then she seemed to relax, and we walked more slowly so I could sniff as much as I wanted.

We went to visit a dog named Zeke and a cat named Annabelle. They lived in a house with a nice big backyard, and Zeke, who was small and black and had short legs, loved to race around the grass and dart under the bushes. Of course I chased him. When I flopped panting to the grass, he would run over and bow with his rear end high, his wiry little tail whipping back and forth. So I'd get up and chase him some more.

It was wonderful!

Annabelle lived mostly inside, although she came out now and then to walk along the top of the fence, which was not fair at all, since Zeke and I couldn't do that. When we met, she sniffed at me once. I loved her breath; it smelled delicious, like fish. So I licked her face from the chin to the ears.

Annabelle pulled back from me and then turned and walked slowly away with her tail high. I didn't mind. If she wanted to play, she could come out in the backyard with me and Zeke anytime.

A girl named Trish lived at the house, too. She was quite good at belly rubs. Her parents stayed there, too.

We visited Zeke and Annabelle for two days, and then we went to a new house. This one had no dogs or cats at all. The next house had an old dog, who mostly slept, and a young dog, who didn't like me to chew on his toys.

In each house there was a girl CJ's age. And some other people, too.

It was glorious to meet all these new dogs! The people were usually friendly, too. And I loved it that CJ often slept on the floor, in a sort of sack that was made of silky, rustling material, very good for burrowing into. It was so easy for me to sleep next to her. No troubles about jumping up on a bed. I'd just walk in circle until the cloth was all squashed down, and I'd curl up with a happy sigh, pressed against CJ's side.

I loved our new life. But I sometimes missed Trent and Rocky and wondered if we'd be going to see them soon.

One day CJ stuffed all her things into her backpack, and we went to a new house. There was a boy there, smaller than CJ, whose hands smelled like the two rats who lived in a cage in his room. He loved me instantly, which I could understand. He didn't have a dog of his own, and rats just aren't as good. Even if you do have two of them.

The boy's name was Del, and we played Tug on a Stick and Chase the Ball in the front yard. Sometimes

CJ watched, and sometimes she stayed inside the house, talking with a girl she called Emily.

This was a good house. I especially liked the space under the big dining room table. I would settle in with my tail near CJ's feet and my head near Del's, because the most delicious treats kept dropping from his lap down to the floor. Bits of buttered bread, wiggly strings of spaghetti, scraps of chicken skin, even a small round tomato once.

After we'd slept at this house for three nights, I was in my usual spot under the table, licking up a shred of roast beef that had just dropped onto the floor, when CJ pushed her chair back. "Excuse me for a minute," I heard her say, and then she left.

I was busy with the roast beef, so I didn't follow her right away. I figured she'd be back. Who would leave the table for long when those delectable smells were floating around?

"Emily. How long is she planning to stay?" asked Emily's mother.

"I don't know, Mom. But she can't go home right now."

There was a silence. I licked Del's ankle so he'd know I was still there. He giggled.

"What I am trying to say," said the mom in a quieter tone, "is that I know CJ has a difficult home situation, but . . ."

"She can't live here," the father said.

"She's not! It's just for a little while!" Emily said.

"I like her," Del piped up.

"This isn't about liking her, son. It's about what's right," the father said.

"And Molly," Del added. I wagged and pricked up my ears. CJ's footsteps were headed back into the room.

"It's not about Molly, either," the mother said with a sigh. "I like her, too, Del. I like CJ. But this isn't her home."

Nobody sounded happy, which I didn't understand at all. They were all up there with the wonderful food on top of the table. How could they be worried or sad?

"No problem!" said CJ brightly from the doorway. "I was just . . . I mean, I heard from my aunt today. I'm going to stay with her." She pulled out her chair and sat down at the table. "Pass the potatoes, please?" she asked.

"Your aunt?" Emily said. "I didn't know you had an aunt."

"Oh, I'm sorry," CJ said as a big blob of buttery mashed potatoes landed on the floor.

I squirmed over to lick up the treat, hearing CJ's voice. "I'll get paper towels. I'm sorry. Don't bother, I'll do it." Her chair scraped back and her footsteps pattered in and out of the room. Then she dropped down to her knees beside me, under the table.

I wagged, happy to see her, as she used a wad of paper to rub at the damp spot on the wood floor where I'd licked up the potatoes.

After the people had finished eating and were carrying plates and bowls to the kitchen, CJ slipped away to the room where she usually slept with Emily. Even though the kitchen still smelled marvelous, I could tell that my girl needed me. I followed her.

There were two beds in the bedroom. CJ flopped down on one of them. I jumped up with her and she held me, and I felt some of her sadness going away.

Helping CJ be less sad was my most important job. I just wished I were better at it. Sometimes the sad feelings felt as if they were buried so deep inside her they'd never go away.

In the morning, Del and Emily and CJ all put on their backpacks. The mother picked up a purse, and the father took a briefcase. Then everybody went to do school, and I was left alone in the backyard. CJ filled my food and water dishes before she went, so I had plenty to eat, but I missed my girl. When she finally came back, I was so glad that I danced and jumped in a circle all around her.

She had my leash, which meant we were going for a walk! How exciting! "Okay, Molly. Easy, girl," she said, holding me still enough to clip the leash to my collar. Then she took me around the front of the house.

She still had her backpack on, I noticed. And it was full and heavy again, like it had been the first day we'd gone to visit Zeke and Annabelle.

Del came out into the front yard to pat me. "Goodbye, Molly," he said. He was sad. I licked his face.

"Do you want me to go with you?" Emily asked. She was standing at the front door.

"No!" CJ said quickly. "I mean, don't bother. My aunt said she'd pick me up on the corner. She'll be there any minute."

Emily sounded a little worried. "Are you sure you don't want to wait until my mom and dad get home from work?" she asked.

"I can't," CJ said firmly. "But tell them thanks for me. Really, Emily. I mean it. They were super nice to let me stay."

"Okay. See you at school?" Emily asked.

"Sure thing. Bye, Em! Bye, Del!" CJ called. "Molly, come on!"

I gave Del's face one last swipe with my tongue and hurried after CJ. How great to be on a walk with my girl!

We got to the corner and CJ tugged at my leash. "Come on, Molly. She's waiting!" she called loudly.

Then we turned the corner, and CJ's steps slowed.

A slow walk was my favorite kind, because it meant I could stick my nose into every clump of grass and check on what had been there before me. Other dogs? Cats? Rabbits? Squirrels? Raccoons? Possums? It was all so interesting! Then there were also ants to investigate, scurrying in and out of those little mounds of dirt. A few crickets whirred up from under my paws, and I snapped at them, but missed.

It was a wonderful walk.

After we'd gone a few blocks, we ended up in a tiny park with a few benches and a swing set. CJ sat down heavily on a bench and eased the backpack off her shoulders.

"Oh, Molly," she said. "What are we going to do now?"

I sat at her feet and peered up at her face, confused. We were together, out for a walk, on a sunny day. How could my girl be sad? I pressed close to her knees, and she bent down to rub my ears with her hands.

"I wish we could just go to Trent's," she said quietly. "But Gloria would find us in a minute." She sighed.

I licked her nose.

We sat there for a while, until some younger kids came to swing on the swing set and their mom sat down on the bench beside CJ.

"Nice dog," she said with a friendly smile, and she reached over to pet me.

Her hands smelled of cheese and salt and crackers. I licked them.

"Thanks," CJ said. Then she got up and slung her

backpack over her shoulders. I followed her out of the park.

That was the longest walk CJ ever took me on. We never went back to Emily and Del's house. Or our own house, or Trent's, or Andi's place. Or anywhere.

After a while I was even too tired to sniff at the grass or investigate what had been happening under the bushes we passed.

I sat down and looked hopefully up at CJ. Wasn't it time to go home now?

"Oh, Molly," CJ said wearily. She sat down, too, and leaned back against the trunk of a tree.

I lay next to her with a long sigh.

She dug around in her backpack and pulled something out. "Here, Molly," she said softly. "I saved something from lunch." She tore half of a sandwich in half again, and gave me one piece. Bread and baloney! I gulped it down. She offered me a handful of salty pretzels, too, and then she pulled out a banana for herself.

"Yuck," she said, looking at it. It had several brown spots and looked a bit dented. But she peeled it and ate it, tossing the skin under a nearby bush.

She took a bottle of water out of her backpack and poured some in her cupped hand for me to lap. She drank some, too. Then she put the cap back on the bottle and stowed it in her pack again.

"We'll save some for tomorrow," she told me, pulling me onto her lap for a hug.

I lay there, panting a little bit. The treats CJ had given me had dulled my hunger a bit, but my stomach was nowhere near full enough. I hoped we'd go back to a house soon, where there would be a bowlful of cool water for me to lap, and another one full of food for dinner.

A man was walking along the street, wearing jeans and high tennis shoes. "Hey, there," he said when he saw CJ and me sitting together. "You doing all right?"

His voice was friendly. I wagged.

"We're fine," CJ said. She hugged me more tightly. "My dad's going to be here to pick me up. Any minute."

"Okay, cool," the man said. He started walking again.

CJ gave a sigh that was almost a groan. She dug into her pack again and found a sweatshirt, which she pulled over her head. And then she heaved herself to her feet. "Come on, Molly," she said.

Her voice sounded as tired as I felt.

We began walking again, much more slowly than before. The sunlight was starting to fade, and with it the warmth was stealing from the air. The air began to get chilly.

When would CJ decide to take us home?

15

All of a sudden, CJ stopped walking. "There, Molly. Do you see?" she asked.

Even my tail was tired, but I still looked up and wagged when she said my name. She was not looking down at me, though. She stared at a house on the other side of the street.

"Come on, Molly," she said. We started across.

I thought maybe we were going to visit some new dogs. I'd even have been happy to see a cat. But we didn't walk up to the front door of the house. Instead, CJ led me up the driveway. The garage door was open.

CJ made that "shhh" sound again. We went inside.

There was a car there, and some big plastic garbage cans, and a lawn mower, and cardboard boxes stacked up against one wall. CJ hurried over to those boxes and sat down beside them, patting the floor so that I huddled beside her. The cement floor was chilly and uncomfortable, like the floor in that cage where I'd stayed for a night before CJ came to get me. I leaned into my girl for her warmth, and she put an arm around me.

The boxes and the car hid us from the view of the street. But it seemed like a cold and boring place to stay. What were we doing here?

Across the garage from us, a door creaked open.

CJ tensed, her arm clamping tightly around me. I could tell she was afraid. I looked around alertly, ready to growl and bite if my girl needed me to save her.

Very gently, CJ put a hand over my muzzle, her fingers on top and her thumb on the bottom. She shook her head.

Heavy feet clomped down a few stairs. I heard someone pry the lid off a garbage can, and a rustle as a plastic bag of trash was lowered in. But I couldn't see anything. The car, a big blue station wagon, blocked my view of whoever was in the garage with us.

CJ closed her eyes.

I could feel her fear trembling through her, and I wanted to defend her. But I understood that she needed me to be still and silent. This was like playing Be Quiet under the stairs back at our old house. I had to wait until CJ told me it was okay to move and make noise again.

The lid went back on the trash can. The feet clomped up the stairs again. A hand hit a button.

The garage door buzzed and creaked and groaned and began to lower slowly down.

I twitched and jumped in surprise, shaking my head loose from CJ's hand. I couldn't help it. That noise was so loud! But I didn't bark.

The garage door came all the way down and shut us in. Suddenly, it was dark.

I licked at CJ's face in apology for moving when we were playing Be Quiet. We sat together for several minutes. Then, very softly, CJ let out a sigh.

Was the game over? I licked at her cheek again. "Good girl, Molly," she whispered, and her hands relaxed their hold on me. Then I knew I'd done the game right.

There were a few windows in the big door, the one that had lowered down. And there was another in a smaller door that led outside. A tiny bit of light from a streetlight outside reached through those windows, and slowly my eyes got used to it. I couldn't see much, but I could see the boxes and the station wagon. I could see CJ beside me.

She rubbed at her eyes with her hand.

Then she patted the boxes until she found an empty one. Moving very slowly and very quietly, she flattened it out into a square. She set it down on the cement floor and curled up on it, patting the cardboard so that I came and lay down next to her.

CJ pulled out a sweater and sweatpants from her backpack, and used them to cover us up. She put her head on the backpack like a pillow. I curled into her stomach, trying to share as much of my warmth with her as I could. She wrapped herself around me.

She cried a little, quietly, into my fur. And then she went to sleep.

I lay as still as I could, so I wouldn't disturb her. I didn't understand anything that was happening. Why didn't CJ go to a bed to sleep, like she usually did? Or, if she was going to sleep on the floor, why didn't she put out that warm, rustling bag that she sometimes used?

It felt wrong to sleep in this cold garage with its smells of damp cement, oil, and gasoline. Even the fascinating trash with all its delicious smells had been stuffed into a plastic container, where nobody could get to it.

This wasn't the right place to sleep.

Again, I was reminded of those days when we'd played Be Quiet under the stairs all night long. Finally, CJ had come to understand that game wasn't any fun. She'd realized that my place to sleep was in her bed with her. Why had she forgotten?

But I couldn't remind her. I couldn't do anything but stay close all night, keeping her as warm as I could.

*   *   *

Faint morning light leaked in through the windows very early. I opened my eyes, but I didn't get up or move until CJ sighed and then groaned softly beside me.

I wiggled around and licked her face. "Oh, Molly," she said, with love in her voice. She reached up a hand to pat me, and then sat up with another groan. "Oh, Molly, I'm so tired!" she moaned very softly. "Okay, shush now. Stay quiet. We have to get out."

She stuffed her sweatpants and sweatshirt back into the backpack and then crawled awkwardly to her feet. I kept close to her as she went to the small door with a window in it. She twisted a small metal latch, turned a knob, and pushed the door slowly and silently open.

We both slipped out into a chilly, grayish morning.

I hurried over to the grass and squatted to leave a puddle. CJ watched me. "Wish I could do that do," she said.

I tilted my head to look up at her. Breakfast soon?

CJ sighed. She settled her backpack on her shoulders. We walked away from the house and along the sidewalk. Then CJ crouched down and took the bottle of water from her backpack. She drank half of what was left and poured the rest into her hand for me to lap up. But I was still thirsty even when all the water was gone.

We walked some more. Every now and then I licked

at the grass, which was thickly covered with drops of dew. It wasn't as good as a real drink, but it was something.

It seemed very early. There were only a few cars driving on the roads, and most houses were shut up and silent. The light wasn't even very bright yet. But it got brighter by the minute as we walked.

We came to a colorful building, its windows shining with light. The parking lot stank of gasoline and oil. CJ left me tied up outside the door for a few minutes, and I sniffed at fascinating sticky spots on the sidewalk as a few cars pulled into the parking lot. The drivers got out and attached long hoses to the vehicles, then took the hoses off again and drove away.

CJ came out quickly and untied my leash. She knelt down to rub my ears. "Molly, we'd better go to Andi's," she said. "I can't think of anything else to do."

I lapped at her nose, wondering again about breakfast. I kept wondering while CJ took me on another walk, nearly as long as the one yesterday.

My feet became sore from the rough pavement, and my head hung lower and lower. CJ walked slowly, too, and her feet did not lift very high off the sidewalk. My stomach was hollow and empty, and I heard a loud grumble from CJ's belly as well. I glanced up to see her rubbing her hand over her stomach and making a face.

We kept walking.

After a long time, my nose began to catch a hint of a

familiar scent. Dogs. Lots of dogs. My head lifted a little bit, and my tail even swished back and forth a few times. If we were going to play with Andi, there might be something to eat. I needed a good meal, not just a treat. But a treat would be better than nothing.

Finally, I recognized the parking lot of Andi's building. CJ hesitated before the front door, anxiety spiking inside her. Then she took a deep breath and pushed it open. We walked in.

It smelled fantastic. There was Luke and all the other dogs, of course. But even better, I could smell their food. Other food, too. On a table against a wall, there were platters full of round pieces of bread. Some were plain; some were rich and sweet. There were big metal jars of coffee, too. I recognized that smell. Gloria drank it in the mornings.

I drooled and tugged at the leash, but CJ held me tightly.

People were sitting in chairs as usual, and Andi and Luke were playing. She held him on his leash and was leading him up to a lady with short white hair. "CJ?" she called with a puzzled look on her face. "Just give me a minute," she said to the people in the chairs, and she and Luke came over to us.

"I didn't expect to see you at this time of the morning," Andi said, while Luke sniffed me briefly. I hardly had the energy even to raise my nose to him.

"Some of my volunteers can only come before work," Andi went on. She waved a hand at the people in the chairs. "What's up?"

CJ put most of her weight on one heel and shifted back and forth a little. "I just thought, maybe, you'd need some help," she mumbled.

Andi frowned. "Isn't it a school day?"

"Yeah, I'm going. Soon," CJ said. "I just kind of thought . . ."

Her voice trailed off. There was a moment of silence. Luke sat down, bored, waiting for Andi to get back to the game.

When Andi spoke next, her voice was gentle.

"Well, I'm always glad to see you and Molly here, CJ. You know that, right?" CJ nodded. "Why don't you check the dogs' food and water, as long as you're here? And I put out some bagels and doughnuts for the volunteers. Help yourself if you want anything."

After that things were *wonderful*.

CJ put me in a pen and right away brought me a bowl heaping to the brim with food and another one full of water. Her hands were shaking a little when she put them down.

I plunged my muzzle into the food and gulped it down. Then I drank most of the water. When I lifted up my head, I saw CJ slipping over to the table full of food and taking two pieces of the round bread. She ate one in three or four bites while Andi and Luke played with the people in the chairs. She spread white creamy stuff on the other and ate it more slowly. I could feel her relaxing from all the way across the room.

Then CJ left for a little while. I plopped down on the floor of the pen for a rest. When CJ came back, she had her backpack on her back again, and she smelled like food and other dogs. I licked her hands happily and let her snap the leash on my collar.

Andi came over to put Luke into the pen. Now that I was feeling better, I sniffed him properly. He ignored me. Luke was like that.

"Is everything okay, CJ?" Andi asked gently.

CJ nodded.

"Well, let me know if you need anything," Andi said. "And remember something, okay, CJ? You can't run away from your problems. They'll always find you."

16

When we left Andi's, we went on another walk.

I had more energy now that I'd eaten, but even so, I had a hard time believing this. I liked walks, but weren't we ever going to do anything else? Naps, maybe?

CJ stood up straighter than she had before, I noticed. She was walking a little quicker. I hurried, too, so that I could be right next to her feet. She seemed to know for sure where we were going.

After a little while, I did, too.

I began to notice smells I was familiar with. Clumps of grass and corners of mailboxes and telephone poles had been marked by dogs that I recognized. I lifted my head, sniffing deeply, and then I strained ahead, pulling on the leash.

We weren't going to be visiting anymore! We were going home!

By the time we reached our block, I was nearly towing CJ down the street, so happy at the idea that I'd eat from my familiar bowl, nap in all my favorite spots, and sleep again next to CJ in our bed. CJ let me drag her across the lawn and up the front steps.

But then she didn't open the door. I jumped up and put my paws on the door to show her what to do, but she just sat down on the steps and patted her leg so that I'd come to sit next to her.

A little disappointed, I flopped down across CJ's lap. Why were we sitting on the porch like this? Weren't we going inside?

CJ hugged me and rubbed her cheek against the top of my head.

"I love you, Molly," she whispered fiercely in my ear. "And I'll never leave you, I promise. I'll take care of you."

She squeezed me a little too tightly, but I didn't really mind. It was my job; I knew that. To be right there with my girl when she needed me.

"Okay," CJ said with a long sigh. "Okay."

She got up and unlocked the door, and we went inside.

I was so happy to be back at last that I used up the last of my energy dashing around to smell everything I'd missed—the carpet in the living room, where I liked to lie in a particular sunny spot; the corners of the kitchen, where a few crumbs might have collected; the spot where my food and water bowls stood. (Both were empty. I'd remind CJ about that later.) Best of all, there was CJ's bed. I leaped up onto it. The blankets and quilt were pulled up smooth and tight, but I pawed at them and pushed with my nose until they were in a comfortable jumble, as they should be.

Then I jumped down to run back to CJ.

She was standing in the living room, not far from the front door, staring at the wall over the fireplace. "Molly, look," she said slowly. I came to sit by her side, panting, and she reached down to stroke my head.

"It's my painting of you," she said. "The one from the art show. Gloria had it framed? And she hung it up? I can't believe it."

I wagged. My tail thumped into CJ's leg. I nosed at her hand, hanging by her side. More food now?

Then CJ and I both heard a creak as the door swung open.

CJ jumped, turning toward the hallway. I was surprised because whoever it was hadn't knocked or rung the doorbell. It was my job to bark at a person outside of the door or greet that person enthusiastically once he or she came in. Which was I supposed to do this time?

"Gloria?" CJ called nervously.

The person who'd opened the door came into the living room. It was Shane.

"You left the door open," he said, looking at CJ.

CJ took a few steps backward, fear suddenly spiking inside her. I crowded close to her leg. Why was she scared? We were home at last. Everything should be all right now.

Maybe she didn't like Shane's smell, just like I didn't. He usually smelled angry. Right now he smelled worse.

"What are you doing here?" CJ asked, her voice higher than usual.

"I saw you walking with that dog," Shane said. "I followed you. Aren't you supposed to be in school? I'm not, of course. Since I got *expelled*."

CJ was beginning to tremble. "Listen. You have to go. My mom will be home soon."

Shane leaned against the door frame. "Yeah, sure. I'll go. After we have a talk."

"We're not talking," CJ said.

"We are. About school. About that stupid art class. What did you tell that teacher?"

"Nothing," CJ said.

I looked back and forth from Shane to my girl. If they had been dogs, I'm pretty sure they would be growling at each other. But since they were humans, they were just talking.

"Oh, right. *Nothing*. You told her I took that stuff from

her desk, didn't you? Or you wouldn't have gotten off so light. How come I got expelled and you didn't, CJ? Unless you told them everything?"

Shane took a step into the room.

CJ took a step backward, but then she bunched her hands into fists and stepped forward again.

"I don't have to explain *anything* to you," she snapped. "You stole a phone and some money! And now you're mad at *me* because you got in trouble? Like I did something to you? Get real, Shane. And get out!"

On the last word, her voice became a yell.

Shane's anger flared inside him, and I knew what to do. Just as I had with Gus in the museum, I growled. My lips pulled back from my teeth, and all the hair along my neck bristled.

I dropped my head down, letting Shane know this wasn't a game. I began to walk toward him.

Shane backed toward the hall, and I could smell the fear and anger fighting inside him. "Get that dog away from me. We're not done here."

"I told you to get out!" CJ yelled again.

"I'll kick your dog!" Shane threatened.

"I'm calling the police right now!" CJ said, and her voice was high and tight with panic. "Molly, come. Come here!"

I stopped, but I didn't come to CJ's side. I knew I was supposed to obey my girl, but I didn't want Shane to think I was backing down. He needed to know that I'd protect her.

"Stupid little dog like that," Shane said from the hallway. His anger was winning. "I'll show you—"

Someone knocked on the door, and it swung open.

Sheryl was standing on the porch.

I wagged once, to show Sheryl I was still her friend. Then I dropped my tail low to let Shane know I hadn't forgotten him.

"What's going on?" Sheryl asked, looking from Shane to CJ.

CJ lifted her chin.

"Nothing. Shane is just leaving," she said.

Shane glared at CJ. At Sheryl. At me.

"Fine," he muttered, and he turned to the door, pushing past Sheryl.

"And don't come back!" CJ shouted after him.

"Don't worry, I won't!" he yelled. And he began to walk quickly along the street with his head down, his hands jammed into the pockets of his jeans.

Wagging my tail, I hurried to CJ's side. We'd done it! Shane was gone!

17

Sheryl looked out at the street after Shane. "Is everything all right, CJ?" she asked.

"It's fine," CJ said. "He's not going to come back here. Molly showed him."

Sheryl nodded. She looked different, I realized. Her face was thin and tired, and she had on a soft, fuzzy red hat that covered her head closely.

"Are you okay?" CJ asked her awkwardly. "I mean . . ."

Sheryl smiled. "Yes. I am okay, CJ. That's what I came here to tell you. Can we sit down?"

CJ nodded, and they sat together on the couch. Since Gloria wasn't here, I jumped up on the couch and laid my head across CJ's knees. I understood the rules—I was a bad dog if I got on the couch while Gloria was home, but a good dog if I did it when it was just me and CJ.

Sheryl looked up at the wall above the fireplace. "Your painting looks good there," she said.

CJ ducked her head. "My mom had it framed," she said in a low voice.

And then the two humans did more of that talking.

I simply did not understand why people thought it was important to spend so much time making noise. Even dogs (most of the time) only bark when there is a reason to bark. Maybe people do it because they are just not that good at playing. Even CJ didn't like to chase and wrestle the way Rocky did.

I closed my eyes and dozed, still tired from all the long walks CJ and I had taken. My ears twitched every now and then, and I heard snippets of the talk going back and forth above my head. "No cancer left," Sheryl said. And, "The doctors say it looks very good." And, "If they hadn't caught it so early, it would have been much worse."

"I have you to thank for that," Sheryl said, and I could hear the smile in her words. "You and Molly."

She reached over to rub my ears. CJ patted my back at the same time. I sighed a long, happy sigh without opening my eyes. Somehow I felt like a very good dog.

I was so comfortable that I didn't even stir when I heard the door click open. A familiar smell, flowery and sweet, flowed in. I knew who it was. I didn't need to bark.

But when CJ went tense all through her body, I opened my eyes and lifted up my head. Then I remembered how to be a good dog now that Gloria was home, and I jumped down from the couch.

Gloria stopped in the doorway, her hands full of shopping bags. She stared. She blinked.

"You're here?" she said.

CJ nodded. "I'm here," she answered.

"I didn't expect to see you." Gloria set the bags down at her feet.

"I guess running away from my problems didn't really work," CJ said.

Sheryl frowned. "Running away?"

"CJ has been living with some of her friends for the past few weeks," Gloria said coldly.

Sheryl looked even paler, and her eyes grew wide.

"You mean she ran away?" She looked at CJ. CJ twisted up her finger in the hem of her T-shirt.

"Kind of. I guess," she said. "Me and Molly."

Sheryl looked shocked.

"But . . . but Miss Mahoney, why didn't you let the school know? Did you call the police? CJ, are you all right?"

CJ nodded. Gloria leaned down to pick up her bags again. Her face looked warm and red.

"Well, there was no need to panic," she said impatiently. "Obviously, CJ was fine. Obviously. And now she's back."

CJ squared her shoulders. She lifted her chin.

"That's right, I'm back," she said. "With Molly."

"Clarity June!" Gloria plopped her bags onto an armchair and turned to face CJ. "You cannot start all that over again. That dog is dangerous."

I lay down on the carpet and sighed. How could CJ have forgotten that my food and water dishes were empty? How long would it take for her to remember to fill them?

"Molly is *not* dangerous," CJ said firmly. "She was only protecting me." Her voice got lower, and I don't know if Sheryl or Gloria could hear the words she mumbled next. "Somebody has to."

Sheryl was looking back and forth from CJ to Gloria.

"Molly, dangerous? I had Molly in my art classes for weeks, and she never showed any sign of being aggressive," she said. "If CJ says Molly was protecting her, I'm sure that's the truth. Molly is CJ's most important friend in the whole world." She lifted her head and looked up at the wall over the fireplace. "You can tell how much she loves her by her artwork. Look at that painting. CJ needs Molly. Don't you want your daughter to be happy?"

Gloria turned to look at the painting, too.

"Well, of course. Of course I do," she said, and her face had grown even warmer than before. "What sort of mother wouldn't want her own daughter to be happy?"

"I'll stay home this time," CJ said into the silence that followed. "I'll stay if Molly can stay, too."

I thumped my tail against the carpet a few times when I heard my name, to remind CJ that there was a hungry dog here who needed attention.

Gloria let out a soft, frustrated snort through her nose. "Well," she said. "Well, I suppose. If the dog has to stay, it can stay."

CJ slid from the couch to the floor to hug me tightly. I panted and licked at her cheeks, waiting patiently for her to feel better so that she could let me go.

After some more talking, Sheryl got up to leave. CJ went to the door with her, and of course I went, too. It was one of my jobs.

"You can always come and talk to me if you need to," Sheryl told her. "And you'll come back to art class, right? With Molly?"

CJ nodded.

"Good. And, CJ? What do you think about individual art lessons?"

CJ's mouth opened a little, but she didn't say anything.

"On Saturday mornings, maybe? At my house. And you can bring Molly, of course. It'll be my way to say thank you to both of you."

A slow smile spread over CJ's face. "That's . . . that's great. I'd like that."

"It's a plan, then." Sheryl gave CJ a quick hug and left.

I looked up at CJ, standing in the doorway, and whined. Food now?

Thank goodness CJ remembered. "Oh, Molly, you poor thing, you're still hungry," she said, and she rushed to the kitchen to fill my bowls up with food and water.

Finally!

CJ didn't go to do school at all that day. She ate a lot at the kitchen table and dropped scraps down for me, and then she took a shower while I waited for her, sitting on a towel she'd laid down for me over the cold tile floor. Sometimes I stuck my nose in between two plastic curtains to see what was taking her so long.

Then she and I took a long, glorious nap in our own bed, and I was so happy I had to squirm up under CJ's arm to lap at her face. She groaned and pushed me away, but I could tell my girl was happy, too.

We napped some more. When we got up Gloria and CJ talked again. But my girl wasn't upset and didn't need me, so I busied myself digging an old ball out from under the couch.

I finally got it and, panting happily, pulled my head out from under the couch to show my prize to CJ.

"Yuck," Gloria said.

CJ shook her head. Just then the doorbell rang.

I ran and barked, doing my job, even though I'd rather have played ball with CJ. Then I got a whiff of a familiar smell through the crack under the door, and I barked more loudly. An answering bark came from the other side of the door.

CJ pulled the door open. Trent and Rocky were there!

I leaped out the door to tackle my brother, and we ran around and around the front yard in dizzy circles, so happy to see each other we couldn't even bow properly. CJ and Trent laughed and chased us, too, joining in the game. How wonderful to be playing with my brother and my two favorite people!

Finally CJ and Trent won the game, CJ by grabbing my collar and Trent by snatching Rocky's leash. They took us around to the backyard, where Rocky and I started to play all over again, tearing around the yard, ripping bits of grass out with our claws, doubling back and pouncing on each other, leaping up to run some more.

This time Trent and CJ did not play with us. They sat on the steps to the back door, talking. More talking!

After I'd pinned Rocky and let him up a few times, we had to break off our game to rush back to his boy and my girl. Rocky stuck his nose in Trent's ear. I lapped at CJ's face.

That got their attention in a satisfactory way. CJ smoothed both of my ears back and kissed the top of my head. Trent gave Rocky a good belly rub, even though he had to let go of CJ's hand to do it. Then my brother and I got back to playing, and our boy and our girl kept on with their talking.

As I jumped on Rocky's head, I looked over at them and saw Trent reach over and take hold of CJ's hand again.

Author's Note

More About Cancer-Sniffing Dogs

Molly's Story takes place in the remarkable world of cancer-sniffing dogs. To research the topic, I turned to a close friend named Dina Zaphiris, because Dina actually trains dogs to detect cancer. In many ways, her dog Stewie provided the inspiration for the book!

When Dina was a little girl, she wanted nothing more than to have a dog. She dreamed of playing with her dog, of grooming her dog, and teaching her tricks. But Dina's parents would not let her have a dog. They did not think it would be a good idea, since they had chickens. So Dina trained the chickens. She taught them to do tricks and to come when she called them by name.

Today, Dina is an adult and has her own dogs. She is a certified animal trainer and was one of the first people in the world to train dogs to sniff for cancer. Dina's dogs do not sniff people directly, as Molly does in the book.

Instead, they sniff fluid samples, usually condensed breath, in test tubes. Dina trains them to signal when they detect the presence of cancer cells. They will stop and paw at the test tube with the cancer, as if hitting it for being bad!

Cancer-sniffing dogs love their work and feel that they are doing something important. After all, helping people is a dog's purpose!

W. Bruce Cameron

Molly's Story:
A Dog's Purpose
By W. Bruce Cameron

Ages 8-12; Grades 3-7

Molly's Story: A Dog's Purpose Novel describes the life of a mixed breed dog from her birth in the home of a kindly woman who fosters strays; to her puppyhood with CJ, a young girl with a difficult home life; to the discovery of her talents as a cancer-sniffing dog and a loyal companion. This fast-paced story of how an unwanted pup and her lonely "girl" help each other find their talents will warm readers hearts while encouraging them to reflect on what it takes to build a strong, supportive family.

Reading *Molly's Story: A Dog's Purpose Novel* with Your Children

Pre-Reading Discussion Questions

1. Titles in the Dog's Purpose series explore the ways canines partner with and support human beings.

What roles do dogs play in your life, and in the lives of your family, friends, and community members? List any other books or articles you have read, or any television programs or movies you have watched, about dogs helping humans. What abilities do dogs have that makes them especially helpful to humans?

2. *Molly's Story* begins in a home where a woman fosters stray animals. What ways might a dog become a stray, or find itself in an animal shelter? What might be some situations in which it is not the best plan for a family to adopt a pet? What are some issues a family might discuss before making the commitment to adopt a pet?

Post-Reading Discussion Questions

1. *Molly's Story* is narrated by Molly, the dog, herself. How does the dog's perspective impact the objects described and the way human discussions are understood?

2. In chapter 1, Jennifer uses the phrase "foster failure." What does this mean? What other insights does Jennifer have about dogs and people?

3. How does Molly feel when she first sees CJ? Does CJ have permission to adopt Molly? What actions does CJ take when she brings Molly home?

4. Who is Gloria? What does Gloria do that makes her seem like an imperfect parent? Several times in

the story, Gloria tells CJ that her behavior is "embarrassing." Is it, in fact, CJ who is behaving poorly in these situations? If you were Gloria's child, how do you think you would feel?

5. Why does a truant officer come to CJ's home in chapter 5? How does the truant officer's visit change CJ's daily life? How does it change Molly's life?

6. Who is Shane? How does CJ meet Shane? How does Shane get CJ into trouble in chapter 9? What advice might you have given CJ about trusting Shane? What reasons can you imagine for Shane's behavior and choices?

7. In chapter 10, as part of her community service, CJ meets a researcher named Andi. What does CJ do for Andi? What does CJ learn about Andi's research? What does Molly learn? Compare the way Molly learns Andi's lesson with the way she learns to stay quiet in CJ's basement earlier in the story.

8. What difficult events in chapters 11 and 12 make having her picture selected for an art exhibit a less than happy occasion for CJ? How do these events involve Gloria, Gus, and Sheryl?

9. What mean trick does Gloria play in chapter 13? How does CJ find Molly and figure out what Gloria has done? What does CJ feel forced to do after she brings Molly home? How do CJ and Molly survive for the next few days?

10. At the end of chapter 15, Andi tells CJ, "You can't run away from your problems. They'll always find you." Do you think this is good advice? How does CJ react to Andi's words?

11. How does Sheryl help save the day at the end of chapter 16? What good news does she give CJ in chapter 17? Where does Sheryl spot CJ's painting? How might this be a hopeful sign for CJ's relationship with Gloria? What agreement does Sheryl help CJ and Gloria make with each other?

12. Through her family troubles, and inspired by her love for Molly, CJ discovers an artistic talent. In what ways might this surprise discovery help CJ over time? Do you have an artistic or athletic outlet, such as drawing, singing, dancing, playing soccer, or running, that helps you work through strong emotions? Do you think it is important to have such an outlet? Why or why not?

13. Although, in the story, Molly often tries to protect CJ, could it be that CJ's desire to protect her dog helps her learn to care for herself? Why or why not? Cite examples from the story in your answer.

14. After reading *Molly's Story: A Dog's Purpose Novel,* how might you describe a pet dog's most important purpose in one sentence?

Post-Reading Activities

Take the story from the page to the pavement with these fun and inspiring activities for the dog lovers in your family.

1. DOG DIETS. Molly reacts to the strong salty taste in ham, and is sickened by eating old food. Dogs benefit from healthy, appropriate diets just like people. Imagine you have a small, part-poodle pup such as Molly, or another dog of your choosing. Visit the food section of a pet store, talk to a veterinarian, or do online research to create an ideal meal plan for this pet. (Hint: Visit http://www.humanesociety.org /animals/resources/facts/pet_food_safety.html ?credit=web_id93480558) What are some best-food choices? How often should this pet be fed? What would be some healthy treats? What human foods might be especially dangerous to this dog and how can they be kept securely away? Invite your child to share what s/he has learned with other young pet owners or dog fans.

2. PET VIEWPOINTS. *Molly's Story* is narrated in first person by Molly, the poodle mix. This helps readers understand the dog's point of view and is also a model for helping children see other peoples' and animals' perspectives. Invite your child to describe, using "I," a few minutes in the life of his or her own pet. If desired, invite your child to describe,

using "I," an experience in the life of a younger sibling, parent, grandparent, or friend.

3. HELP OUT. Molly is a lucky dog to have been fostered in a welcoming home and found her way to CJ's heart. Many strays and unwanted pets are not so lucky. Help your child find ways to help these unlucky animals, such as donating to a pet food drive, volunteering at a local shelter, or designing a poster to raise awareness about this problem. Brainstorm poster titles (e.g., FOSTER OUR FURRY FRIENDS or CAN YOU HELP A STRAY DOG?) and information, such as a phone number or web address for a local pet shelter. Organize your art materials, such as poster paper, paints, markers, colored pencils, and/or images found online or cut from magazines. Create your poster. Visit a nearby supermarket, pet hospital, or library with your child and encourage him/her to ask if they have a good spot to hang your poster. Take a photo of your child beside their mounted poster to share with friends and family!

Reading *Molly's Story* In Your Classroom

These Common Core-aligned writing activities may be used in conjunction with the pre- and post-reading discussion questions above.

1. Point of View: *Molly's Story* is narrated by Molly the dog, but other characters' viewpoints are also critical to understanding this story. Have students write a two to three paragraph, first-person account of the day Molly met "her girl," the truant officer's visit in chapter 5, the art class, or CJ's nights spent at friends' houses in chapter 14, from the viewpoint of CJ, Gloria, Trent, Sheryl, or another character.

2. Communities and Relationships: Through their work, both Sheryl and Andi interact with CJ without being able to completely address her difficult home situation. Using details from the novel, write a short report describing Sheryl's art classroom, or Andi's research space. Explain the goals of their programs, and the people they hope to help. Read your reports aloud to friends or classmates. Discuss the ways each program was helpful to CJ. What did CJ and Molly learn? What similar, good qualities do the programs share? Are there programs in your own community that might have been helpful to CJ? How might a young person help a troubled friend or classmate find a helpful class or other resource?

3. Text Type: Opinion Piece. Both Molly and CJ are "strays" in different ways. Write a one-page essay exploring the meaning of the word "stray" and the ways in which this story might be read as two strays' journeys of beating the odds together.

4. Text Type: Narrative. In the character of CJ, write the story of how Molly helped you learn more about true friendship and how this helped your friendship with Trent grow. Or, in the character of Shane, write the story of why you stole from Sheryl, why you got so angry with CJ and, maybe, why you are jealous of CJ.

5. Research & Present: PET HOMELESSNESS. Although Molly is a great help to CJ, the girl and her dog find themselves in several risky home situations during the story. Go to the library or online to learn more about how pets lose their home situations and how this can be prevented. (Hint: Visit http://www.aspca.org/animal-homelessness.) Use this research to create two checklists, one entitled "Are You Ready to Adopt a Pet?" and one entitled "Can You Help Save an Animal from Homelessness?" Have students make copies of their checklists to share with people in their community. If desired, offer copies of the list to be made available at your local library, animal shelter, or pet hospital.

6. Research & Present: CANCER DETECTION & OTHER AMAZING ANIMAL ABILITIES. Molly's actions help Sheryl detect her cancer early, making her treatment more effective. Visit the websites listed at the back of the book to learn more about dogs that may be able to detect dis-

eases or predict seizures, horses that may help with psychotherapies, or cats that may help autistic kids. Have small groups of students create oral presentations about their findings. If possible, have students give their presentations to others in their grade or school.

Supports English Language Arts Common Core Writing Standards: W.3.1, 3.2, 3.3, 3.7; W.4.1, 4.2, 4.3, 4.7; W.5.1, 5.2, 5.3, 5.7; W.6.2, 6.3, 6.7; W.7.2, 7.3, 7.7

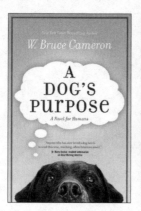
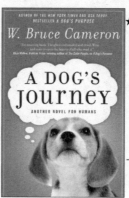
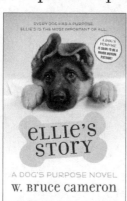
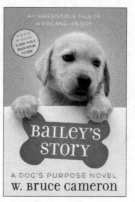

About the Author

W. Bruce Cameron is the *New York Times* bestselling author of *A Dog's Purpose, A Dog's Journey,* and *The Dogs of Christmas.* In addition to *Molly's Story,* his books for middle-grade readers include *Ellie's Story: A Dog's Purpose Novel* and *Bailey's Story: A Dog's Purpose Novel.* He lives in California.